Praise for *Saint Louis Armstrong Beach*

"Brenda Woods captures all the sad and radiant glory of New Orleans in her exquisite *Saint Louis Armstrong Beach*. She ably uses the Hurricane Katrina tragedy to open up large themes of love, loyalty, and the eternal power of music. Highly recommended."

—**Douglas Brinkley**,
historian and author of *The Great Deluge: Hurricane Katrina, New Orleans, and the Mississippi Gulf Coast*

"This is a lovely read—funny, heartbreaking, thoughtful and fluid. I felt like Woods took us right into New Orleans, right into the eye of the storm and the heart of New Orleans' people. I can still hear Saint's horn, still can see his smile and closed the book just wanting more."

—**Jacqueline Woodson**,
Newbery Honor–winning author of
Feathers, After Tupac and D Foster and *Show Way*

"Brenda Woods' story is satisfying and full of hope, a hope that resides in the strength and resilience of the people of New Orleans, but most especially in the tender heart of Saint Louis Armstrong Beach, who, by story's end, has a new and deeper song to play on his clarinet."

—**Nikki Grimes**,
Coretta Scott King Medal–winning
author of *Bronx Masquerade*

also by brenda woods

A Star on the Hollywood Walk of Fame
My Name Is Sally Little Song
Emako Blue
The Red Rose Box

SAINT LOUIS ARMSTRONG BEACH

brenda woods

Nancy Paulsen Books 🌀 An Imprint of Penguin Group (USA) Inc.

NANCY PAULSEN BOOKS
A division of Penguin Young Readers Group.
Published by The Penguin Group.
Penguin Group (USA) Inc., 375 Hudson Street, New York, NY 10014, U.S.A.
Penguin Group (Canada), 90 Eglinton Avenue East, Suite 700, Toronto,
Ontario M4P 2Y3, Canada (a division of Pearson Penguin Canada Inc.).
Penguin Books Ltd, 80 Strand, London WC2R 0RL, England.
Penguin Ireland, 25 St. Stephen's Green, Dublin 2, Ireland
(a division of Penguin Books Ltd.).
Penguin Group (Australia), 250 Camberwell Road, Camberwell, Victoria 3124,
Australia (a division of Pearson Australia Group Pty Ltd).
Penguin Books India Pvt Ltd, 11 Community Centre, Panchsheel Park,
New Delhi—110 017, India.
Penguin Group (NZ), 67 Apollo Drive, Rosedale, Auckland 0632, New Zealand
(a division of Pearson New Zealand Ltd).
Penguin Books (South Africa) (Pty) Ltd, 24 Sturdee Avenue, Rosebank,
Johannesburg 2196, South Africa.
Penguin Books Ltd, Registered Offices: 80 Strand, London WC2R 0RL, England.

Published simultaneously in Canada.
Printed in the United States of America.
Design by Annie Ericsson.
Text set in Goudy Old Style.
Library of Congress Cataloging-in-Publication Data is available upon request.
ISBN 978-0-399-25507-6
1   3   5   7   9   10   8   6   4   2

In memory of my great-grandparents—
Lee Murphy and Henry and Alabama Jordan—
and my grandparents—John and Josie Jordan—
who once called the city of New Orleans home.

And to my mother, Maxine,
a member of the graduating class of
1940, McDonogh No. 35 Senior High School,
New Orleans, Louisiana.

THE STORY OF SAINT LOUIS ARMSTRONG BEACH

One thing I know for sure is that most important stuff comes in more than one part. Things like skateboards, bicycles, computers, houses, cars, and life. Life is made out of this invisible thing called time that we watch disappear into weeks, years that we track like bloodhounds or K-9 dogs, and centuries that move so slowly they may as well be standing still. The last time I checked on my computer, 616 weeks had disappeared since the day I was born, which makes me almost twelve but technically still eleven.

Other stuff has a beginning and an end: red lights and green lights, the muddy Mississippi River, clarinet lessons, the road to Lake Pontchartrain, summer vacation, video games, and life. Life always has a beginning and always an end.

As for me, my life has three parts: the before, the during, and the after. My before was mostly good and the after keeps getting better every day, but the during sure was hard. The during was, I hope, the most horrible-est thing that will ever happen to me. The during was almost my end.

The during is also known as Hurricane Katrina.

This is the story of Saint Louis Armstrong Beach. No, it's not a place with folks trying hard to catch a big-enough-for-dinner fish, or where big-mouth pelicans and noisy seagulls swoop. And it's not a place where I paddle out too far on my Boogie Board, come face-to-face with a ginormous wave that looks like it wants to swallow me, and even though I know I shouldn't take the ride, I do anyway and luckily land belly-up on the sand in a pile of dead smelly seaweed.

No, Saint Louis Armstrong Beach isn't one of those places. Saint Louis Armstrong Beach is me. And like I said, this is my story, beginning with the absolute best day of my mostly good before—August 20, 2005—exactly one week and two days before the during.

THE ABSOLUTE BEST DAY
OF MY MOSTLY GOOD BEFORE

"Saint, shut that dang dog up!" my pops yelled from his bedroom.

"His name's not Dang Dog," I muttered.

The sun was up and so was I because Shadow was outside barking. Shadow is the neighborhood dog, the kind that belongs to everyone but no one in particular. Pops calls him the noisiest dog in Tremé, but that's not even close to the truth because Tremé has its share of noisy dogs. And for those of you who don't know much about New Orleans, Tremé is just *back* from the French Quarter and the way you say it is *Trah-MAY*.

Anyway, Shadow was yelping and scratching at our back door like he did every Saturday, which had somehow turned into my day to feed him. I stretched, rolled out of bed, and headed downstairs.

My hand was still on the doorknob when he pushed his way inside, jumped up on me, and started licking my face, his tail swishing like a windshield wiper. Shadow may belong to everyone on our block, but I swear I'm his favorite. Whenever he sees me outside, he runs straight to me, an arrow to a bull's-eye. He's coal black, mostly Labrador, we think, and if I could, I'd own him. But Pops keeps saying no because when he was a kid a dog bit him twice, right on the butt, and since then he's had it in for canine creatures. As for Shadow, he seems perfectly happy with things just the way they are, never being cooped up, no collar around his neck, no tags jingling, free to follow behind anyone he chooses—like a shadow. That's how he got his name. In fact, it was me who gave it to him . . . well, me and my used-to-be best friend, Money Lafayette.

Quickly, I opened two cans of dog food and scooped it into his bowl, but before he stuck his nose in it, Shadow gazed up at me with a look that lets me know I'm his friend. I patted him and opened the fridge to see if my pops, Valentine, had brought anything special from the restaurant.

Having a pops who's a chef at a famous restaurant is good in one way but bad in another. It's good because he usually brings home leftover fancy food and it's bad because my mouth has kind of gotten used to it. I searched the racks, nothing special today, so I settled for cereal.

As soon as I finished eating, I got dressed and grabbed my clarinet and cowboy hat. "See y'all later!" I called out from the landing to my mama and pops.

Mercedes, my mama, appeared in the doorway of their room, tying her robe, fussing with her hair. Her hair and eyes are black and her skin's the color of peanut butter. She's not skinny or fat and she smiles with her whole face. "You be careful, Saint!" she said. "And be home way b'fore dark," she added.

"I will."

"You got some change?" she asked.

I checked my pocket. I had three quarters and seven dollar bills. Hopefully by the end of the day I'd have a lot more. "Plenty," I replied.

Mama made the sign of the cross, kissed her fingertips, and tossed me a blessing.

I caught it.

Mama smiled. "Love you."

I grinned. "Love you too," I replied, and thought about how lucky I am that my mama and pops never nag me about spending most of my spare time performing and are very cool about me being into music. But they weren't always like that.

The summer before sixth grade, when I'd asked if I could start performing in Jackson Square, I got a double no. So I told them I signed up for advanced swimming lessons at the park, a little white lie, and instead headed to Jackson Square with my clarinet. And I got away with it too—for four days, that is.

On the fourth day, I was playing to a small crowd of happy tourists, really putting on a show, when I glanced up and there they were, Valentine and Mercedes Beach, not smiling. How they knew where to find me I'll never know. My punishment consisted of having to actually take advanced swimming lessons and no street performing for a whole year.

"A whole year? You gotta be kidding!" I argued. "Do you know how much money I could be making?"

"Take it or leave it," they'd replied.

Surprisingly, the year seemed like it passed in no time, and now I'm a really good swimmer and also free to put on the Saint Louis Armstrong Beach Show practically whenever I want.

Shadow trailed me to the front door and I had one foot outside when I saw her climbing into the passenger side of her mama's car. "Hey, Money!" I shouted, hoping for the hundredth time that she'd talk to me or at least smile. Instead, she glanced my way, frowned, waved at me like she was shooing away a fly, and shut the door. I imagined her whispering the words *little boy* as her mother drove off and watched until the car turned the corner. Shadow, resting on his hind legs at my feet, was quiet and as still as a statue. "C'mon, boy," I told him, and headed to the Quarter. Like a shadow at noon, he was on my heels.

"Mornin', Saint," old Miz Moran greeted me from her narrow porch, where she was sitting in her creaky rocking chair like she does every day but Sunday. Sundays she goes to early mass at St. Augustine's, then takes the Canal Street ferry across to Algiers to visit her daughter. Come Monday, though, you'll find her right back in that chair, creaking and watching, watching and creaking.

"Hey, Miz Moran."

"I ever tell you that you're as handsome as that tall, brown daddy of yours?"

Almost every time I see her, she says the same thing. "Yes, Miz Moran."

And as usual she shook her crooked finger at me and chuckled. "You be good as a saint, now."

"I will," I promised, knowing I couldn't, wouldn't ever come close to being any kind of saint . . . well, maybe in my dreams . . . naw, not even there.

As I walked, I once again wished that my name wasn't Saint. Folks always have something to say about it—and I mean always. Usually they assume my pops is a huge fan of the New Orleans Saints, which he is, but that's not how I came by the name. Then, I wished my middle name wasn't Louis Armstrong, but only because the trumpet's not my instrument, and since I carry his name, some people insist it ought to be. If I could have picked my own name, I'd have chosen Valentine Xavier Beach, just like my pops. Instead I was named after my pops' daddy, Saint, who according to everyone who knew him was anything but, and Louis Armstrong, who supposedly had been a bosom buddy of his. King Daddy Saint, which is what almost everyone called him, already had one foot in the grave when I was born, so my mama and pops gave him the honor of naming me. Sadly, six months after I was born, King Daddy Saint died.

Halfway to Jackson Square, I thought about Money again, not the money in my pocket, the Money who lives next door to me and who, even though she's a year older than me and is a teenager now, up until just before Christmas had been my play sister and very best friend.

Her name's not really Money, it's MonaLisa, but a long time ago her baby cousin who couldn't say MonaLisa started calling her Money and it stuck. That's another thing that happened last year. She told everyone, "Please stop calling me Money. Call me MonaLisa." But . . . I never did.

Shadow nudged the back of my leg as if to say stop thinking about her, but I kept on.

The way I figure, there are three reasons Money changed up on me. The number one reason was that she got her girl parts, which caused the older boys in the neighborhood to glance her way and sling sweet talk. The second reason was that she grew at least five inches in what seemed like overnight, making her a full head taller than me. The last reason was her parents let her transfer from St. Anne's, our Catholic school, to the public middle school last fall. In no time flat, she became a member of this pretty-girl clique who kept on her about why the *little boy* was always hanging around her house. "Hey, *l'il boy*," they teased, and whenever Money was with her new friends, she began to ignore me. But if she was alone, she'd still talk to me when I'd knock on her door or squeeze through the back fence into her yard, so I didn't mind too much, and Mama said, "Don't let your feelings get hurt, Saint. It's just peer pressure." Mama's a social worker at a big hospital, so she knows all about that kind of stuff.

Then, just before Christmas, everything changed.

I rang Money's doorbell and this high school dude with a goatee and a thick gold chain who I'd seen around now and then, always with a different cutie, answered the door like he lived there. Because I'd seen her parents leave for work, I'd expected her to be home alone. Inside, music blasted.

"Is Money here?" I asked.

He smirked and peered inside. "I dunno. Lemme see.

Is Money here, y'all?" he yelled over the music. I peeked through the cracked door. It was a party. People were dancing. I recognized some of the girls from Money's clique.

"Naw, money ain't here, but if you got some you wanna give us, you welcome to c'mon in," one of the fellas replied. By that time people were laughing, so when the brother with the goatee threw the door open as if to say it was okay to enter, something warned me not to, but I didn't pay attention. Instead, I listened to the nosy side of me and stepped inside.

There were open liquor bottles on the coffee table and almost everyone was drinking. I scanned the room for Money.

"It's *li'l boy*," one of the girls slurred, and took a sip from her paper cup. Snickers followed.

Then this blue-eyed Creole brother poured some alcohol into a cup and handed it to me. "Here . . . have a taste, *li'l boy*."

He and some of the others began to cheer me on and I had the cup to my lips when, from the corner of my eye, I glimpsed Money coming downstairs, a bottle in each hand. Without taking a sip, I lowered the cup from my mouth.

"The *li'l boy* wanna know if Money's here," the high school brother told her.

As soon as she saw me, she tried to hide the bottles behind her back.

"H-hey, Money," I stammered.

"My name ain't Money, it's MonaLisa, everyone knows that," she proclaimed, then asked, "What're you doin' here, Saint?"

That really got them started. "Saint . . . Saint who?" the blue-eyed brother asked.

"Saint Beach," I replied.

Even more laughter.

"MonaLisa's *li'l boyfriend*," one of the girls mocked.

The one with the goatee glared at me as he slipped his arm around Money's waist. "That so?"

"He's just a kid from next door . . . a kid from next door who needsta go home . . . now," she commanded as she quickly ushered me to the door.

"Bye, *li'l cutie*," the girl with the paper cup said, and her giggling followed me outside.

Before Money closed the door in my face, she glanced at the cup that was still in my hand and grabbed it. "Gimme that! And Saint, keep your big mouth shut. Don't turn into no rodent on me or I'll never talk to you again, ever."

I gazed into her pretty brown eyes. "I won't," I said, and left.

Later that day, Shadow must have heard the sad song I was playing on my clarinet. He squeezed through the gate into the backyard and nuzzled my shoulder like he wanted to play. At least he's still my friend, I thought.

That should have been the end of that story because, as promised, I kept my big mouth shut.

It was Money who didn't.

Christmas Eve, Money's mama, Miz Olympia Lafayette, came to our house wearing a lot of makeup, a glittery green dress, and, instead of her usual perfect smile, a disgusted look. She burst in like a mad bull. "Where's your mama, boy?"

Boy? She'd never called me boy before, always Saint. "What's wrong, Miz Lafayette?"

"'Tween me and your mama."

I pointed to the kitchen, where Mama was getting the roux started for her gumbo.

Miz Lafayette rushed through the house, her high-heeled shoes going click, click, click, click on the wood floors, and closed the kitchen door. Next thing I knew, I was summoned to the kitchen and ordered to sit down. Like detectives on a lady cop show, Mama and Miz Lafayette began their cross-examination.

To make it short, when Miz Lafayette went to the locked cabinet to get the liquor out for her annual Before Midnight Mass Party, which was supposed to start any minute now, it was all gone.

"At first Money played stupid," Miz Lafayette snarled. "But she finally told the truth."

I hung my head. "Oh."

"Saint, look at me," Mama commanded. "This true?"

I nodded.

Miz Lafayette patted Mama's shoulder sympathetically. "Don't know how any one person could go through that much liquor, let alone an eleven-year-old."

"Huh?" I asked.

"Your drinking problem . . . Money told me everything. How you tried to get her started but—thank the Holy Blessed Virgin—she wasn't weak."

My ears couldn't believe what they were hearing. I spit out the truth. "Me? It wasn't me. It was Money and her friends. They were all at your house. I just went over there to see if Money wanted to go with me to get something to eat, and she was havin' a party. That's who was drinking, not me. I didn't even take a sip."

Miz Lafayette's eyes shifted from Mama to me, then back to Mama again.

I peered into the front room at the painting of my grand-daddy Saint that hangs over the fireplace mantel, placed my hand over my heart, and declared, "I swear on King Daddy Saint's grave, I'm tellin' the truth."

For some reason, I still can't say why, Miz Lafayette believed me. She retreated to the front of the house and we were right behind her. "Sorry to have bothered y'all on Christmas Eve." She paused briefly, then added, "Y'all welcome to come by t'night."

Mama begged off. "Gotta get my gumbo on, Olympia."

"Then I'll see y'all at midnight mass."

"Like always," Mama replied.

"Merry Christmas, Mercedes . . . you too, Saint. Sorry," Olympia Lafayette apologized again, and she scurried home.

"Merry Christmas," we echoed.

Mama shut the door and plugged in the Christmas tree lights. The tiny white lights twinkled and the yellow glass ornaments sparkled. Every year Mama's trees had a color theme. This year's was yellow.

She lifted up my chin and gazed into my eyes. "Not even a sip, Saint?"

"Not even," I replied.

Playfully, she rubbed my head. "C'mon, help me with the shrimp."

Though the shrimp wouldn't go in until minutes before the gumbo found its way to the bowls, it needed to be shelled and cleaned tonight. Most times Pops did it, but he'd called earlier, saying he'd probably be at the restaurant until after 1:00 A.M.

I peeked through the window curtains at Money's house, where I could hear Miz Lafayette screaming at her, but as soon as the first partygoers rang their bell, she stopped. Even though I was mad at Money for lying on me, I still felt sorry for her. I let the curtain fall and joined Mama in the kitchen.

Hours later, at midnight mass, Money stood to get in the Communion line, but Miz Lafayette made her sit back down. On my way down the aisle to the altar, I caught Money's eyes. They were red from crying and filled with hate.

Money hasn't spoken to me in the eight months since.

I felt like I was being cooked inside an oven, heat coming at me from every side. Shadow was panting and sweat dripped from my forehead. As usual in August, it was way too hot. I tiptoed into someone's yard and plucked a ready-to-burst pomegranate from a tree that had so much fruit, I convinced myself it wasn't really stealing. And when I passed in front of Willie Mae's Scotch House, I smelled red beans cooking. When my work is done, I thought, I'll stop there for fries and lemonade.

On Moon Walk, across Decatur Street from Jackson Square, I set up. Moon Walk in the summertime had three things I needed: tourists, a few shady trees, and the Mississippi River breeze.

First, I found a container I could put water in for Shadow and filled it at one of the drinking fountains. He lapped it up fast, so I filled it again, then took a long drink myself. I tossed my cowboy hat on the ground, threw in a couple of rocks to keep it from blowing away, opened my case, and took out my clarinet. I imagined the hat full of change and dollar bills and me studying at Juilliard someday. With Shadow curled nearby, I began to play.

Rule Number One: Always start early.

I learned that from the one and only Smokey De Leon. Like a priest is a man of the cloth, Smokey De Leon is a man of the flute, at least that's what he told me. "Knew the flute was plenty trouble first time I put my lips to it. That was the day I forgot about everything else. Some days I'd even forget to eat. Woulda forgot 'bout women if they hadn't chased me night and day." And when folks ask him how long he's been playing, he gazes into the sky dreamily and tells them, "Seems like fo'ever." He's kind of skinny, probably from not eating, and he's got a head full of white hair and grown-up grandkids, which makes him—old.

According to Smokey, tourists who've been warned to steer clear of some parts of New Orleans at night feel safe strolling almost anywhere in the morning. Plus, he claims, you get them with their wallets full, before they've had a chance to spend too much money in the Old French Market or along Royal Street or in the Bourbon Street bars.

I stopped playing and listened. Behind me the Mississippi water quietly rushed and the wind carried the sound of a flute to my ears. My eyes searched the Walk. Though I couldn't see him, the man of the flute was near.

Then, in the distance, I saw them, three folks strolling toward me. Guessing they were tourists, I put my green Cecilio clarinet to my mouth and blew some blues.

While one smiling tourist lady pointed her camera in my face and took lots of pictures, a bald-headed man wearing shorts and a sun visor that had the words *New Orleans* printed on it in bright red letters tossed a couple of dollars into my hat. The other grinning tourist lady, wearing strands of Mardi Gras beads and chomping a praline, stuffed in a five-dollar bill. Inside, I chuckled. The day was off to a very good start. And as soon as I was alone, I snatched the crisp five-dollar bill, folded it neatly, and put it inside the secret money pouch I keep taped around my ankle.

Smokey De Leon's Rule Number Two: Never let folks see you with too much money.

There are two reasons for this rule. First, folks with money might think you don't need any more and pass you by, and second, folks who don't have much themselves might try to rob you.

Sweat dripped into my eyes. I wiped at it with my white handkerchief, did some addition in my head, and realized that if things kept up the way they had for most of the summer, I'd soon be able to call it mine—a beautiful Leblanc

L1020 Step-Up Pro clarinet. One of Smokey's friends who he used to play with at the Jazz Park was selling off some of his instruments and had promised it to me at a discount, $1200. He also has a Leblanc 1191S Opus II, but he wants $5000 for it. Mr. Hammond, my music teacher, claims that's much too much money for a young person to spend on an instrument. I'd say he's probably right.

A daydream fell into my mind, and I was picturing the Leblanc L1020 in my hands, when someone tapped me on the shoulder. Startled, I jumped. It was Smokey. Shadow howled long and loud.

Wearing a purple button-down shirt, faded blue jeans that were way too big, black suspenders to keep them from falling off his skinny body, a red bow tie with yellow polka dots, and a gray derby, he looked ready for Mardi Gras. The hat, which I've never seen him without, matches almost perfectly the color of his eyes, which is why everyone calls him Smokey. "Dreamin' 'bout that Leblanc, ain't ya?" he asked as he settled on the bench, flute, as always, in his hand.

I nodded. "How'd you know?"

Smokey grinned. "The look in your eyes. I know that look."

"Another two hundred dollars and it'll be mine," I boasted.

"Congratulations, Mister Saint," he replied before he placed the flute to his lips and began playing the birthday song.

"It's not my birthday yet, Smokey."

Swaying to the melody with his eyes closed, he continued playing until the end. "Nosiree, it's mine," he proclaimed.

"You jokin'?"

"No sir, Mister Saint, no joke. Seventy-nine today, August 20, 2005."

"Seventy-nine? Wow, that's old."

Smokey agreed, "Yep, gettin' there. Never thought I'd see the twenty-first century, but here I am."

Part of me wanted to talk hogwash and tell him he didn't look his age—you know, that stuff grown-ups always say—but Smokey has gray hair and a bunch of wrinkles. In other words, he really does look old, and I wasn't in the mood to tell a lie. Besides, I have a one-white-lie-a-day rule. Pops claims white lies don't hurt much, but Mama says a lie is a lie. I didn't know who was right, so a while back I decided to allow myself one white lie a day and only if necessary. The way I figured, it wasn't even noon yet and I didn't want to waste a lie I might need for later. So instead I said, "Well, happy birthday, Smokey," and proceeded to play the birthday song for him on my clarinet.

He stood in front of me, put his hands together, and bowed. "You gettin' pretty good with that thing, Mister Saint. Keep it up and one day you'll be a virtuoso."

"What's a virtuoso?" I asked.

"A master of his instrument . . . but remember what I taught you."

He'd taught me a lot of whats. I shrugged my shoulders. "Which what?"

"Music ain't nuthin' 'less you put your soul in it."

"Is my soul in it?"

"Almost." He winked, put the flute to his lips, began to play, and strolled away.

"Bye, Smokey," I said with a wave of my hand.

Abruptly, he stopped playing, turned to me, tipped his hat, and replied, "No such thing as good-bye for me and you, Mister Saint." With that, Smokey resumed playing and sauntered away toward Jackson Square.

Something about Smokey always left me smiling, and that's what I was doing when a herd of tourists showed up.

"Got a song for us?" one of them asked.

I nodded. "This is for Smokey De Leon, a friend of mine," I told them, and played the birthday song again. And when someone asked me for another song, I gave them an all-time tourist favorite, "When the Saints Come Marching In." Then a Mozart piece, which as usual raised some eyebrows. I followed it with "Summertime" by Gershwin. They were impressed by my versatility, I could tell. By the time they left, my hat was brimming with bills. Quickly, I stowed them in my pouch.

"That Leblanc is 'bouta be mine," I told Shadow.

Shadow yelped.

Almost like a whisper, I heard someone calling out my name. There were people milling around and I searched their faces for someone I knew. Then, four times in a row, "Saint, Saint, Saint, Saint," each time louder, a girl's voice, until finally *she* stood right in front of me. "Saint!" she screeched. It was a girl from my class whose name is Jasmine Jupiter. Most people, including me, call her Jupi, but some call her Star Girl because she knows two tons of stuff about astronomy. You know, planets, constellations of stars, even stuff about other galaxies. I'm kind of indebted to her because she helped me study for the planet test and even taught me how to remember them in their order from the sun—My Very Educated Mother Just Served Us No Pizza—Mercury, Venus, Earth, Mars, Jupiter, Saturn, Uranus, Neptune, Pluto. Jupi's latest thing is palm reading, which she swears can predict the future. Her skin and eyes are a pretty chocolate brown and her hair is always in braids. And somehow she's always showing up where I am.

"I'm not deaf, Jupi."

Jupi stared at me with that twinkle in her eyes she always has whenever we're alone. "Sorry."

It isn't breaking news that she likes me. She is way too obvious.

21

"What're you doing here?" she asked.

I held up my clarinet.

"Still trying to make money for that Leblanc?"

"Yeah. I only need another two hundred dollars," I informed her.

"Let's go, Jasmine!" someone yelled. It was her pops.

I waved hello.

"In a minute," she hollered, then sweetly commanded, "Lemme see your hand so I can read your palm."

Figuring it was just an excuse for her to touch me, I gave her my hand. At first she was smiling. Jupi looked extremely cutie-licious when she smiled. But suddenly, she frowned.

"What?"

"Nuthin'," she said softly.

I stared at my own palm like I knew what to look for. "Don't lie, Jupi. You saw somethin' . . . what?"

"I swear, it's nuthin'," she repeated. "Plus, you'll get mad."

What I saw in her eyes made me feel creepy, like the way I felt last Halloween when I snuck into the St. Louis Cemetery No. 1 after dark with some of my buds. I pleaded, "You can tell me . . . whatever it is. I promise not to get mad."

She held my hand again and blurted, "You have a very short life line."

"Which means?"

"You're probably not gonna live much longer."

I yanked my hand away. "Shut up, Jupi! You dunno jack! I can't stand you!"

Jupi hung her head. "Sorry, Saint," she whispered.

"You can leave . . . now," I ordered.

Shadow bared his teeth and growled at her.

"Sorry," she repeated, and headed to where her pops was waiting.

When she glanced back at me, which I knew she would, I gave her the evil eye. Jasmine Jupiter, Jupi, Star Girl, whatever you want to call her had freaked me out.

I examined the lines on my palm closely and wondered which one was the life line. Bunch of black magic, voodoo, hocus-pocus, I told myself, remembering the stuff I'd heard my pops say about palm reading and fortune-tellers. Besides, if Smokey could live to be seventy-nine, so could I. Better yet, I'd live to be ninety-nine and hope Jupi was still around so I could tell her, "Told ya you didn't know jack. What you gotta say now, Star Girl?"

A clump of tourists surrounded me, forcing me to stop fuming and get back to business. They looked like the sort that only wanted jazz, and that's exactly what I gave them. But while I was playing, I thought about having told Jupi "I can't stand you." Well, there goes my lie for the day.

. . .

Its job almost done, the sun began to set. "C'mon, boy," I said, and headed toward home. Shadow wagged his tail happily and tagged along. The Mississippi River was quiet and I'd quit expecting a cool breeze hours ago. Even without the sun, it was still August hot.

My take for the day was ninety-eight dollars and some change, an all-time record. "If those still mimers hadn't shown up in the afternoon, I woulda made even more," I grumbled to Shadow. Even so, I was shining like a five-hundred-watt lightbulb inside and out.

Most Saturdays, I take a detour along Bourbon Street, watching the tourists, waving at some of the carriage drivers who know me, peeping into the bars, including the Jazz Shack that King Daddy Saint used to own, but today I decided to avoid the crowds in the Quarter. And as I made my way home, I tried to persuade myself to forget about Jupi's prediction. "What does she know, anyway?" I asked Shadow. Like he was agreeing, Shadow yelped.

By the time I passed Willie Mae's restaurant it was dusk, and I decided not to get the fries and lemonade I'd promised myself, but only because I didn't want to hear it from Mama if I came in after the streetlights came on. She has these special buttons I try not to push too often. Her *she's going to holler at me so long, I'll wish I didn't have ears* buttons. Me coming home after dark was one of those buttons.

Thinking back to Jupi's prediction, I glanced at my palm and wondered who Mama'd fuss at if I was dead. Probably at me, for dying. Just a buncha hocus-pocus, I reminded myself.

Before I opened the door, I smelled the corn bread baking. Pops' car wasn't in the driveway, so I let Shadow follow me inside.

Mama peeked from the kitchen. "Thank you for gettin' in before dark."

I tipped my hat.

"How'd you do?" she asked.

"I only need a hundred and two more dollars," I told her proudly.

"That's terrific, Saint. Dinner's almost ready and your pops should be here soon, so you'd better feed Shadow in a hurry and put him outside, you hear?"

"I hear. Lemme put my stuff away first." My stuff included my money, which I keep in a makeshift safe inside a secret compartment in my closet. Only one other person in the cosmos knows about it—Money Lafayette. So if any bills ever turn up missing, I know exactly who to accuse.

But in case Jupi's right about this life line thing, maybe I should leave Mama and Pops a note, I worried. It'd be a shame to leave this much cabbage to turn into dust. *Stoppit, Saint. Jupi doesn't know jack.*

Later that night, I was upstairs in my room playing video games when I heard noises coming from outside—someone crying loudly. I poked my head out the window. At first it was quiet, then suddenly more boohooing. Immediately, my ears locked in on the source, the Lafayettes' backyard. It was Money. I rushed downstairs, tiptoed past the living room where my parents were snuggled together watching a movie, and snuck outside. She was still blubbering.

Softly, I called from my side of the fence, "Money?"

She kept crying.

I tried her real name. "MonaLisa?"

The crying stopped but she didn't utter a word.

"You okay?" I asked, pulling the loose fence board we used to climb through aside so I could see her.

"Go away, Saint," she sniveled.

"Whatsa matter? Did someone die?"

"Yeah, me." She started wailing again.

Like an eel, I squeezed through the fence into her yard, half expecting her to make a beeline inside, but she stayed on the top back porch step, hunched over, sobbing away. Cautiously, I settled on the bottom step.

"You don't look dead to me," I told her. Some of me felt

26

sorry she was so upset, but most of me was glad she was talking to me again.

She wiped her snotty nose with her sleeve. "I may as well be."

"Are you sick?"

"No!" she blurted. "I'm 'bouta run away."

"Where to?"

"Anywhere."

"How come?" I asked. It was a question I kind of knew the answer to. She was still grounded.

"Cuz it's been eight months since . . . I still can't have no cell phone, no computer. When school starts again, Mama or Daddy gonna still be taking me to school and soon as the bell rings be picking me up like some kinda armored truck drivers."

When she said that, I started laughing because her name is Money. Get it? Armored trucks . . . money pickups.

She squinted her eyes. "You think that's funny?"

I shook my head. "No, definitely not funny."

"And all summer, my nana's been making me read the Bible to her for hours, claims she can't see the words. She needs to get some glasses and soon," she rambled.

"Oh."

"Yeah, oh. It's prison . . . like I'm under house arrest. May as well have one of those ankle things on. Juvie'd be better'n this. Can't go nowhere. Can't hardly talk to no one. All I got is can'ts."

"Oh," I repeated.

"That all you got to say, 'oh'?"

"No . . . I mean, eight months is a long time."

"Feels like eight years." She paused and started boohooing again. "Darius, the dude with the goatee, kicked me to the curb. Said he didn't have time for no little girl," she whimpered. "I ain't even got no friends no more."

"You got me," I told her, hoping it was true.

"You don't get it, do you, Saint?"

I shrugged.

"That clique was *all about the cool.*"

"Kinda like me, right?" I said, attempting to make her smile. It worked and she grinned. "Wrong."

"You sure?" I asked, inching up to the next step. "Cuz today I made almost a hundred dollars' worth of cool."

"Money don't make you cool."

"So what does?" I asked, and pushed myself up to the step where she was sitting.

"Cool is all 'bout how you talk, how you walk, how you dress, how you be."

"Like I said before . . . kinda like me."

Finally, Money laughed. "You so crazy, Saint." She leaned into me and rested her head against mine.

Us being together again felt like heaven, and if this wasn't heaven, it sure ought to be.

Out of the blue, she did something that totally amazed me. With one hand, she turned my face toward hers and kissed me on the cheek but almost on the mouth. Afterward, Money leaned her head back on mine. I took this to mean that we were on good terms, but right then I didn't feel like her play brother anymore. This new feeling like a gazillion fluttering fireflies had gotten inside of me. Silently I wished she would kiss me again—this time square on the mouth. Only she didn't. She just said, "And stop callin' me Money, okay?"

"Okay."

Like a tree, I was still planted there when Shadow showed up, wriggled into her yard, pranced up the steps, and began licking our faces. We were doing some crazy giggling when Shadow let loose one of his famous killer farts—farts worse than someone who'd just finished off two plates of red beans and rice.

Money held her nose. "Pee-yuu!"

"Maybe we should have named him Fart," I said.

"For real," she replied.

And that night, before I fell asleep, I decided that even with Jupi's palm-reading nonsense, August 20, 2005, Smokey De Leon's birthday, had turned into a day that was better than any birthday I'd ever had. It was the absolute best day of my life. The absolute best.

IN THE PALM OF MY HAND

Sleep had won and the sun had snuck up on me. I rubbed my eyes and stretched.

"You still in bed, Saint?" Pops asked. He was standing in my doorway, dressed for church.

"Gonna be late for mass!" Mama hollered. "You know how I feel about being late for mass!"

"Better get a move on," Pops warned.

I shot past him into the bathroom.

"Don't some people die in their sleep?" I asked my parents as we drove. I'd started a mental list of possible ways I might bump into Mr. Death.

"Some," Pops answered. "Why?"

"Just wondering."

"Oh," he replied.

"Can love really make you sick?"

"What?" Pops asked.

"You know, lovesick," I explained.

Mama chuckled. "It's just a saying."

"That's good," I said, then asked, "But if a person had an incurable disease, they'd know, right?"

"Maybe," Mama answered.

"And suppose someone was going to be in an accident. Do you think they'd have a . . . what's it called—a premo—?"

Suddenly Pops took his eyes off the road and glanced around at me. "A premonition?" Ahead, the stoplight turned yellow, then red. Pops screeched to a stop.

"You need to drive more carefully! You could kill somebody!" I blurted loudly.

"What's wrong, Saint?" Mama asked, and touched my forehead with her hand, checking to see if I had a fever. "You feeling okay?"

"Yeah, I'm cool."

"Then why all these questions?"

"Just curious."

She stared into my eyes and raised one eyebrow like she didn't believe me.

For the next few blocks I didn't say a word. Then, as we were turning into the church parking lot, I saw a guy who looked like he was homeless holding a sign with printed words that said THE END IS NEAR—REPENT. He looked right at me and grinned.

I gasped and made the sign of the cross.

And as if I was truly jinxed, we wound up sitting in a pew right behind Jupi, her two big-head younger brothers, and her parents. With smiling faces, they turned and greeted us.

"None of us know how much time we have left on this earth," Father Collins preached from the pulpit.

Huh?

"None of us," he repeated.

Except for me, Saint Louis Armstrong Beach, who, according to Jasmine Jupiter, will sometime in the very near future croak!

The priest continued, "Therefore, we would be wise to make good use of our time in this world."

After a few more minutes of his boring words of wisdom, my mind dissolved into nothingness—a clear plastic bag of air. And the next thing I knew, the congregation was on its feet and folks were reaching toward my hand, saying, "Peace be with you."

Jupi extended her hand to me. "Peace be with you, Saint."

I slipped my hand into my pocket and scowled at her. *Kiss my donkey.*

"Sorry, Saint," Jupi whispered as I stood in the doughnut line in the church basement after mass.

"You ain't got nuthin' to be sorry for," I told her.

"Why?"

"Cuz I've got big plans for the future and I'm gonna live to be a hundred, maybe a hundred and ten," I said confidently.

"You could," she agreed.

If she was trying to turn me into a nutcase, she was doing a good job. "Didn't you just tell me yesterday that I was 'bout to bite the dust?"

"Maybe I was wrong. Meet me at the library tomorrow at ten o'clock on the dot."

"For what?"

"I bet they have better books on palm reading than the really old one I found at my auntie's house. They have books about everything."

If Jupi really was wrong, I needed to know so I could stop worrying. "What library?"

"The one on Loyola between Tulane and Gravier."

"Okay," I said, and took a chomp out of my doughnut.

The next morning, Mr. Lafayette was outside, watering his (as he calls it) hopeless grass. Mondays were his day off. "Hard to keep anything green in this heat."

"I spoze."

"Where you headin' in such a hurry, Saint?" Sometimes he liked to talk and this was one of those sometimes.

"To the library."

Just then, Money opened their screen door and waved. "Hey, Saint."

I halted and gave her my cool-little-brother-head-tilted-to-the-side nod. "Hey, MonaLisa." I'd practiced saying it over and over last night, hoping I wouldn't screw up.

"Where you goin'?" she asked.

"To the library," her pops answered.

In a flash, she was standing in front of her pops. "Can I go?" she begged. "Pleeeeze?"

The look on his face had me convinced the word *no* was about to come out of his mouth, but probably because most parents want their kids to hang out in libraries, he instead said, "To the library and nowhere else, y'all promise."

We gave our word and vamoosed.

MonaLisa was what my gramma in Baton Rouge calls tickled pink. She tugged my arm. "Let's go to Willie Mae's."

"No . . . I gotta be at the library by ten. Plus, if anyone sees you there, you'll be sentenced for life." I sped up.

"Yeah, yeah, yeah . . . you're right." She paused, then asked, "Why're you goin' to the library?"

"For a book—about palm reading."

34

By the time we got there, I'd told her the whole story.

"Tell me you don't believe in that booty cheddar."

"Booty cheddar?"

"Crap."

"Not really."

"Then why are we here?"

I shrugged.

Jupi was waiting out front.

"Hi, MonaLisa," Jupi said with a squint that let me know she wished I'd come alone.

"Hey, Jupi."

"I got here early and already looked at some books. It's not as simple as I thought."

"It's a buncha booty cheddar," MonaLisa blurted.

Jupi's eyes jumped from MonaLisa to me. "Huh?"

I interpreted. "Crap."

"Maybe so, maybe not," Jupi replied.

"And by the way, Jupi—isn't it 'bout time you made everyone call you Jasmine?" MonaLisa asked.

Jupi twisted her mouth. "I dunno. C'mon."

We tagged along behind her up the stairs. "There are lots of books." Jupi opened one and pointed. "The name for all this stuff is palmistry, and the people who practice it are called palmists. Look, this picture shows hand shapes. There are four kinds, earth, air, water, and fire."

"Sounds just like astrology. God's gonna send both a y'all straight to hell," MonaLisa scolded.

Jupi chewed at her nails. "We're just learnin'. No sin in that."

"Yeah," I agreed as I studied a diagram of the palm lines in one of the other books. Instantly, I zeroed in on the one called the life line and matched it to mine. Jupi was right; my life line was short, real short. I gasped and sank to the floor.

"Gimme that!" MonaLisa demanded, and yanked the book from my hand. I was in a daze. Minutes passed. "Told y'all this was nuthin' but nonsense. It says right here . . . 'The length of the life line isn't linked to how long a person will live.'"

I sprang to my feet. "Show me . . . where?"

"Right here. It says a long time ago palmists used to believe that, but they don't anymore."

Like a speed reader, I scanned the paragraph, then belly laughed. "That's exactly what it says!" I proclaimed loudly.

Jupi smiled shyly, rested her hand on my shoulder, and gazed into my eyes. "I told you my auntie's book was really old." She paused and her eyes twinkled. "And for once I'm really glad I was wrong."

"Now can we go to the teen section and look at some real

books or magazines even?" And like a snake, MonaLisa slithered away.

Quickly, Jupi and I placed the books back on the shelves and strode after her.

It was just after noon when Jupi's pops picked her up.

"You ready to bounce?" MonaLisa asked me.

"Yeah, let's roll."

"She's cute," MonaLisa remarked as we strolled.

I knew exactly who she was talking about, but I still asked, "Who?"

"Jupi."

"I know."

MonaLisa poked my shoulder. "Plus, she's diggin' on you," she teased.

"Yeah, I know."

"A lot."

I chuckled.

"I'm comin' back to St. Anne's for eighth grade. My mama 'n' daddy are makin' me," she said matter-of-factly.

To music only I could hear, I started doing the Saint Louis Armstrong Beach boogie, a little hip-hop mixed with my famous pop-locking.

"Stoppit, Saint! You look too stooo-pid."

But I was in a groove and I kept dancing until I accidentally brushed against her. Suddenly, those gazillion fireflies got inside me again. I remembered Saturday's almost-real kiss and shivered. Love?

When we got home, Mr. Lafayette was still working in his yard, clipping his hedges. His face, back, and armpits were drenched with sweat. He wiped his forehead. "So, where's the library books?" he asked.

"We were just doing research," MonaLisa replied.

Right away, that look that gets on grown-ups' faces when they think you're lying got on his. He asked three questions. "Research? In the summertime? On what?"

Without a thought, I answered, "Palm reading."

Then another grown-up look got on his face, the one that makes you think you said something in a foreign language. "Oh" was all he said.

The question-answer thing seemed over.

"Me and Saint are goin' inside to make a sandwich, okay?"

He nodded and inquired, "Palm reading?"

MonaLisa rolled her eyes and blurted, "Saint has a short life line, so he thought he was gonna die, but we found out he isn't. Can we go now?"

"Yeah. And if y'all make tuna, don't use too much mayonnaise and save some for me."

MonaLisa squinted shiftily. "I could make you some lemonade, Daddy," she offered. I could tell she was trying hard to get off punishment for good.

But Mr. Lafayette was smart and he gave her that other grown-up face that says *I'm not as stupid as you think.* "Lemonade would be nice . . . not too sweet."

"I know."

Of course, I was given the job of lemon picker and squeezer.

"Use the strainer to make sure there's no seeds. He hates that," she bossed.

But I didn't care. I'd squeeze a whole treeful of lemons if she asked me.

She put the sandwich, lemonade, and a plate of cookies on a fancy tray and brought it to her pops. "Am I still on lockdown?"

Mr. Lafayette grinned. "Don't seem like lockdown to me. Y'all went to the library and Saint's here. Don't push your luck, Miz Money."

I waited for a comeback but there wasn't one. She'd let him get away with calling her Money.

In a little-girl voice she asked, "Can I have my computer?"

He took a sip of lemonade. "Ask your mama when she gets home."

"What about my cell?"

"Ask your mama. . . . Did y'all clean up behind yourselves?"

"We will . . . then can I at least go over to Saint's house?"

When her dad said no, MonaLisa scowled and stormed into her house. I was right behind her. She must have cussed for ten minutes straight.

The next day, she was shipped off to her nana's house again, I supposed for more Bible reading. Mrs. Lafayette was one tough warden. The lockdown continued.

HURRY-CANE

One hand was on the front doorknob and my clarinet was in the other when Pops asked, "Where you headin'?"

"To Moon Walk, maybe the Quarter. I almost have enough to buy the new clarinet."

"Not today, Saint."

"How come?"

"Storm supposed to hit the Florida coast."

"This ain't Florida."

"Might change course is what I'm hearin'. Most big storms seem to have minds of their own."

"A hurry-cane?" I asked, saying the word the way I had when I was little.

"Tropical storm. . . . Katrina."

41

Remembering last year's Hurricane Ivan and the seven hours it took for us to travel eighty miles to my gramma's house in Baton Rouge, I sighed. "Tell me we're not gonna have to evacuate again."

"I dunno. But what I do know is that your mama'll have nine kinds of fits if I let you outta my sight. Later we'll go on over to Lil Dizzy's for some lunch and I'll drop you off at the hospital with your mama on my way to work. Those are my orders."

"Dang!"

Pops raised an eyebrow.

"I said *dang*."

He gave me his *be careful Saint* stare.

"Can I at least go outside?"

"Yep."

I opened the door and scanned the sky. Except for a single straggly cloud, it was clear and bright blue. Meteorologists can be wrong, I thought. But just in case, I dashed upstairs to find my list.

Saint Louis Armstrong Beach's Evacuation List

1. My clarinet
2. My money
3. My computer

4. The 18K gold engraved cuff links and tie clip King Daddy Saint left me
5. My video games
6. Shadow
7. Extra boxer shorts

During the Ivan evacuation we'd been in such a rush that I'd forgotten some very important things. Plus, Mama had the car so stuffed that there was barely a spot for me, let alone my clarinet and computer. So after Ivan I'd made the list and strategically figured out a way to arrange everything in one of those plastic storage boxes—everything but Shadow, of course.

It had taken two bucketfuls of tears to get Pops to agree to bring him with us, and even though I'd found Shadow with time to spare, for some reason I couldn't get him to follow me. So I had to leave him. But as soon as we returned home after Ivan, I'd bought a leash and collar. That way, if we ever had to evacuate again, I'd be the boss of Mr. Shadow. I dragged the storage box out of my closet. The leash and collar were still inside.

I went to my computer and typed in the words *Tropical Storm Katrina*. There it was. A tropical depression had turned into Tropical Storm Katrina near the Bahamas.

Hurricane warnings had been issued for southeastern Florida. If it turns north and west, as some were predicting, Katrina might hit Mississippi and Louisiana.

Pops came in and stood over my shoulder, staring at the monitor.

"We could get lucky. Maybe it'll fizzle before it has a chance to gather enough energy to do much damage."

"I got my fingers crossed that it doesn't reach New Orleans."

"Get your things ready today just in case, Saint," he ordered.

"What about Shadow?" If he said no, I was prepared to whine, blubber, and snivel.

But without any hesitation he replied matter-of-factly, "Okay."

"For real?"

"For real," he echoed.

"Thanks, Pops," I said as I whipped around in my chair, but lickety-split he was out of the room. Something smelled fishy. That was way too easy. I didn't even have to use my pitiful look. He's probably betting on a repeat of last year. Trying to outslick me, huh? I glanced at the storage box and chuckled. The collar and leash would remain my secret. Still, I needed a plan of action to make sure Shadow would be around. In no time at all I had one, but I needed a sneaky accomplice—MonaLisa, of course.

Our garage has a classic 1956 Chevy inside that Pops has been working on for as long as I can remember. His *project,* he calls it. *Heap of junk* is Mama's name for it. Every other inch of space is taken up by bits of this and that. Stuff we might use someday. But MonaLisa's garage is always empty. Pops claims it's because they like to keep their expensive cars outside for everyone to notice. I don't care. An empty garage spells temporary doghouse.

Today, I thought, as soon as I get home with Mama, I'm heading to MonaLisa's house pronto. She has to help me. After all, I am her only friend while she's on lockdown.

THE PLAN

1. Find Shadow today.
2. Use the collar and leash to capture him.
3. Put him in MonaLisa's garage with his food and water.
4. Walk him twice a day so he can poop.

That way, if we did have to evacuate, I'd know exactly where Shadow was. I had it all figured out.

Of course, as with almost every tricky scheme, there was a flaw. MonaLisa said yes. I found Shadow. And with food and water, we hid him in her garage. Where he barked all—night—long.

The next morning, when the doorbell rang at 6:00 A.M., no one had to tell me who it was: Miz Lafayette.

All I heard her say was, "Take this animal."

Then I heard Pops apologize.

Then I heard the door close.

And then I heard, "Saint!"

I'd forgotten one thing, a muzzle.

"Sorry, but I knew you wouldn't let him stay here."

"You're right. Darn dog barks all night."

"His name's Shadow," I reminded him.

"Folks gotta get some sleep."

"If we let him stay inside, he might not bark." We both knew it was a lie.

And so, as I let Shadow off the leash to roam, I lost a small battle. But the war wasn't over.

Problems to Solve
1. How to get a muzzle.
2. Where to keep Shadow.

Instantly, I had the answer to number one. When Pops dropped me off at Mama's work, I'd take a quick detour to the pet store that was right around the corner. Now for problem number two. For the next few minutes the circuits in my brain worked hard until I finally got it the answer—old Miz Moran, the neighborhood animal lover. She always puts food out for stray cats and she loves her some Shadow.

"Okay if I go see how Miz Moran's doin'? See if she needs

some help?" I asked Pops. Helping old people is only one of many ways to build a parent's pride.

As expected, Pops' eyes beamed that *I'm so glad you're my son* look. "Sure."

"Thanks, Pops." I grinned and scurried to Miz Moran's.

"Hey, Miz Moran. Came to see if you need any help packing in case we have to evacuate."

"I'll tell you the same dang thing I told my daughter this mornin'. I ain't goin' nowheres. Me and everythin' I own is stayin' right here. Watched 'em build them levees 'long Pontchartrain after that storm in '47. Hurricane cain't scare me. Lived through Betsy. After that, they built them levees up to twelve feet. Only evacuated once for Cah-mille becuz my mister made me. And even that one turned and missed New Orleans. B'sides, won't be long b'fore they put me in the ground no way. So you g'on back home and tell your daddy it's very nice of him to send you over here, but I ain't budgin'." She balled up her fist and shook it at me like she was prepared to fight. She was mad.

"No one sent me. I came on my own."

Her face changed and she gave me the *you are such a nice young man* gaze.

If I hadn't been doing this for a good cause, I would have felt like a crumb.

"You hungry, Saint?" she asked. "Got some crab cakes I could heat up, and fruit punch."

I licked my lips. Crab cakes, it was the least I could do.

"Takes a while for my old oven to heat."

"Don't you have a microwave?" I asked.

She pointed to an unopened box in the corner of her front room that said MICROWAVE OVEN. "Been sittin' there for years. Got no use for none a that. Woulda gived it to the Goodwill but it was a Christmas present from my daughter."

While Miz Moran fiddled in the kitchen, I looked around. Though I'd been inside her house more than a few times, it felt like I'd never really seen it. I scanned her wall of mostly old black-and-white photographs and landed on one of a smiling couple on their wedding day. It had to be Mr. and Miz Moran.

She peeked from the kitchen. "The one next to that is me and my sis, MiMi, at one of the Mardi Gras balls. Lord, we used to have us some good times during Mardi Gras."

"Yeah, Mardi Gras is fun," I agreed.

"It ain't nuthin' like it was back then. Mardi Gras was somethin' you planned for. All the balls. The dresses. Lord, it was wonderful."

Usually I hate it when old people start to talk about the good ole days, but today with Miz Moran I let it slide.

I was washing down my third crab cake with punch when

I decided to come clean. "I didn't really come over here to help you pack."

"You don't say."

"I came to ask you for a favor."

She didn't seem surprised. "That so?"

"Thank you, Miz Moran," I told her a half hour later as I hovered at her front door. Problem number two was solved. "Soon as I get the muzzle and find Shadow, I'll bring him over."

As usual, she wagged her finger. "Be good as a saint now, you hear?"

"I hear."

"And you welcome to stop by anytime to visit and have a li'l bite to eat. Old folks gets lonely."

"I will," I said, then I headed home. And when I glanced back, she was still on her porch, looking after me. If Hurricane Katrina did come and we were ordered to evacuate New Orleans, I hoped she'd change her mind.

As soon as I got home, Pops ordered me to the car. "Gonna drop you off with your mama before I head to the restaurant."

I needed cash for the muzzle. "Can I at least go to the bathroom?"

"Be quick."

Because the Leblanc was almost mine, I really didn't want

to spend any money, but I had no choice. I had no clue how much a muzzle cost, so I took five twenties from my safe, snatched my duffel bag, and scrambled.

"So Miz Moran's gonna evacuate this time, huh?" Pops inquired as we drove.

"Nope," I replied. "Said she wasn't goin' anywhere."

"Then what were you doin' there so long?"

"She made some crab cakes."

"Were they good?"

I rubbed my stomach. "You know it."

Pops and I joined in laughter.

"Traffic's starting to get heavy," he noted. "Lotsa folks are already leavin' the city, just in case."

"But the levees'll keep most of the water out, won't they?"

Pops sighed. "Hope so."

He dropped me off in front of the hospital. "Your mama's in the cafeteria waitin' on you," he said, and sped off.

As soon as he turned the corner, I made a beeline to the pet store. And minutes later, when I greeted Mama, the muzzle was in my duffel bag and I was grinning.

"You look happy," she remarked.

"I am."

The rest of the day was spent trailing her from place to place, sitting in on a boring meeting where people in charge of the hospital were reviewing the hurricane preparedness plan. Mama called these *if* meetings. *If* this happens, then we do this, or *if* that happens, we do that. They seemed to have it all together, but some had worried faces.

"There's nothing to be concerned about. Remember Ivan?" some doctor commented.

Heads nodded.

"Yeah," I agreed. "We went to Baton Rouge for nuthin'."

Eyes flew to Mama, who quickly glared at me and pressed a finger to her lips, telling me to hush.

"Sorry," I said.

Mama's cell phone rang as soon as we got home. "What now?" she asked.

I figured it was the hospital.

"Yes," she said, and paused while the other person talked. "The patients in the ICU, of course," she answered.

"Can I go to MonaLisa's?" I mouthed and gestured.

"Yes," she mouthed back.

My belief that the best time to try to get away with stuff is when parents have their minds on other things had been confirmed twice today.

"You gonna evacuate if they tell us to?" I asked MonaLisa as we searched Tremé for Shadow.

"We're leavin' tomorrow for Los Angeles to go to my auntie's wedding. Spozed to fly back Monday. But if they evacuate, we'll stay there till whenever. Y'all goin' to Baton Rouge again?"

"Pro'bly, if they make us."

"Shadow!" she shouted. "Here, boy!"

"Here, boy!" I repeated, and whistled as loud as I could. Still no Shadow.

"My daddy said he's sick of this hurricane mess. We might move to Houston if he can find a good job there."

"Texas?" I asked.

"What other kinda Houston you know?"

"But you can't."

"Why not?"

"B-be-cause," I stammered, then mumbled my pops' words, "because ain't no place like New Orleans."

"For real, huh?"

That was when Shadow, tail wagging, acting like he didn't have a care in the world, found us. Before long we had him on the leash and at dusk deposited him at Miz Moran's.

Her television was blaring with hurricane news. "These weather people sure like to make a fuss, don't they?"

The forecasters were now claiming Katrina might be a major hurricane.

"Sure like to make a fuss," Miz Moran said again.

A JUST-IN-CASE DAY

"Saint!"

I opened my eyes. It was barely morning. I must be dreaming, I thought, until I heard it again, coming from the front yard.

"Saint!" I knew the voice—MonaLisa. I bolted out of bed, practically bounced down the stairs, and stepped outside in my pj's.

"Hey," she said. "Sorry if I woke you up."

"No you're not."

"You're right, I'm not."

"Whatsa matter?"

"Nuthin'. We're leavin' for the airport. I wanted to say good-bye."

"You're comin' back Monday, right?"

"Depends on the hurricane. Some people died in Florida, and they're pretty sure it's comin' this way. My daddy boarded up last night, just in case."

I looked up. The sky was still that beginning-of-the-day gray color.

From his shiny white Escalade, Mr. Lafayette honked and motioned for MonaLisa to come. "Gotta go," she said, and kissed me on the cheek. The fireflies inside me were suddenly wide-awake.

"Mornin', Saint! We're goin' to Los Angeles! My sister's big wedding at the Ritz-Carlton!" Miz Lafayette yelled.

I waved.

MonaLisa grimaced. "She has the biggest mouth on earth. Wants everyone in the neighborhood to know."

I laughed.

"See ya Monday," MonaLisa said, and added, "I hope."

"Me too."

Seconds later they were gone, and I headed to my room to catch the z's that got away.

My head had just hit the pillow when Mama came in and tapped my shoulder. "Saint."

"Huh?"

"Get up and get dressed."

"No, I wanna sleep," I moaned.

"Need you to come to work with me."

I yawned and pulled the covers over my head. "Again? I don't wanna."

"No choice, young man."

Young man? Those were her *I'm serious* words.

"So get up and get dressed now. We have to find other hospitals to send our patients to if they decide to evacuate New Orleans," she explained.

"All right."

We were in the car when it finally occurred to me. "Where's Pops?"

"At the restaurant. He'll be by to pick you up at lunch-time."

For the rest of the drive, Mama was the way she gets when she has too much on her mind—quiet. And when we got to the hospital, I understood why. It was the opposite of calm.

Like a third-grader, I was led to the cafeteria. "You need money for breakfast?" she asked.

I nodded.

She slipped me a twenty. "Eat and plant yourself right here."

"Okay."

"I mean it, Saint," she commanded, then bounded off to problem solve.

It was buffet style and I got scrambled eggs, sausage, bacon, hash browns, grits, toast, milk, orange juice, and hot choco-late. "Hungry, huh?" the cashier asked.

The answer to the question was obvious, so I just grinned.

I was checking out the room for an empty table when I saw my friend, the man of the flute, Smokey De Leon. He was busy with a plate of food.

"Hey, Smokey."

He glanced up and chuckled when he saw the mountain of food on my tray. "So you learned my secret?"

"Secret?"

"A heap of food on the cheap. Hospitals got plenty of it. Have a seat, buddy."

"My mama works here," I explained as I slid into a chair.

"Think you told me that once . . . I think." He shoveled a forkful into his mouth. "She's some kind of—"

"Social worker," I reminded him.

He stared at the television that was mounted to the ceil-ing. Hurricane news blared. "As long as the levees don't get breached, it should be fine."

"You gonna leave if they tell us to?"

"Yes indeed. I'm old, not stupid, Mister Saint. Got a daugh-ter in Atlanta with a big house. Me and my tribe plan to head there if need be."

Smokey must have been a mind reader, because just as I was getting ready to brag about how much I'd saved for the

Leblanc, he asked, "How's that money comin' along for that L1020?"

Taking into account what I'd spent on the muzzle, I was still close to my goal. "I'm just 'bout ready to call it mine."

"Good, cuz I got it right here for you. Been carryin' it around for a couple days, hopin' I'd run into you. Never thought it'd be here." Smokey lifted a clarinet case from the floor and laid it on the table.

"But I don't have all the money yet," I said.

Smokey smiled slyly. "Paid in full is what I was told."

"But—"

"You got a birthday comin' up, don't you?"

"Yeah. I'll be twelve," I replied.

"Consider it an early birthday gift from me to you." He slid the case toward me.

"You bought it for me? Are you kiddin'? That's a lot of money, Smokey."

"Don't you worry. I've been, shall we say, frugal."

My eyes got watery.

He patted the case. "What you waitin' on? . . . Open it up."

I put down my fork and flipped open the case. There it was, a beautiful Leblanc L1020 Step-Up Pro clarinet. "It's really mine?"

"Yessiree."

"Thank you, Smokey. I'll pay you back."

"That won't be necessary, unless the definition of 'gift' somehow changed overnight."

Hurriedly, I put on the mouthpiece and played some scales. It was more than perfect. Suddenly I was on my feet, doing the Saint Louis Armstrong Beach boogie. Every eye in the cafeteria was on me. When I finished, some folks, including Smokey, applauded. I bowed and sat down.

"You should eat b'fore your food gets cold," Smokey said.

But right then I wasn't interested in food. Carefully, I ran my fingers over the Leblanc and sighed. There might be a hurricane coming, I thought, but to me this was one spectacular day.

Smokey glanced at his watch. "Well, Saint, I spoze something called destiny brought us together today, but I promised my son I'd be home where he can find me, just in case New Orleans comes under siege and we are forced to once again retreat. I hope to see you sometime soon." His gray eyes stared into mine. "You take good care of that instrument."

"You know I will," I told him. I stood up and gave him a big hug. "Thanks, Smokey."

"My pleasure," he replied, and with that, he put on his derby and was out the door.

For safekeeping, I rested the case in my lap, then got back to the business of food.

Obeying Mama's order to stay planted wasn't easy, but I

did. And from the cafeteria TV I learned a bunch of stuff about hurricanes, and Louisiana, the Pelican State.

Stuff I Didn't Know About Hurricanes

A. Over the past 150 years, 49 hurricanes have struck Louisiana.

B. The intensity of a hurricane is measured by something called the Saffir-Simpson scale. It goes from 1 to 5, and 5 is the worst.

C. The weight of a single cubic yard of water is equal to 1700 pounds. WOW!

D. The chance of Hurricane Katrina hitting New Orleans head-on was calculated today to be only 17 percent.

I'm no math genius, but 17 percent didn't sound like we had much to worry about, so I gave up watching TV and decided to unplant myself and do some hospital snooping. Besides, my butt was getting sore from sitting so long. I grabbed my instrument and headed to the corridor.

Of course, who did I immediately run into? "Thought I told you to stay planted," Mama said sternly.

Lucky for me, the restroom was close by. "I have to pee." My white lie for the day.

"Excuse me?"

"I have to go to the restroom."

Mama pointed at the bathroom door. "Go," she ordered.

"Can you hold this for me?" I asked, offering her the clarinet.

Her face turned into a question mark. "Did you have this with you this morning?"

"Nope."

"Did your pops bring it to you?"

"Nope." I was having fun messing with her mind, wondering how many more questions she'd ask before she got mad.

But right then, someone said her name over the loudspeaker, "Mercedes Beach, call 4443 . . . Mercedes Beach, call 4443," so she was saved.

"Go to the restroom and then straight back to the cafeteria, or you can come sit in my office with me."

"Can I use the computer?"

"Yes."

"Your office," I decided. Mama was hardly ever in her office. I'd have it all to myself—sweet. I trailed her. And as expected, she was immediately called away.

Before anything else, I took out the Leblanc again and played a few songs. Next, I turned on the computer, but soon I got drowsy, so I curled up on the sofa and crashed, making up for this morning's subtracted z's.

I awoke to Pops standing over me. I yawned and stretched. "Is it lunchtime already?"

"Not yet. But they decided to close the restaurant." His eyes shifted to the new clarinet. "Where'd that come from?"

The Leblanc was cradled in my arms like a baby.

"It's the one I've been saving for. Smokey gave it to me as a gift."

"Gave it to you? Why?"

"He said it was an early birthday present."

"That's an expensive present."

"Stop worrying, Pops, he's not a weirdo or nuthin'. Smokey and me are all about music. It's our destiny. He's like a grandpa."

That seemed to calm him down.

"Okay. C'mon, we need to pack."

As we drove, we shot the breeze.

"Is evacuation mandatory?" *Mandatory* is a word I'd learned this morning from the TV newscasters. It means people have to do something or else.

"Not yet, but it's not lookin' good. We need to be ready just in case."

"But there's only a seventeen percent chance," I argued.

"Of a *direct* hit," Pops said.

"When are we leaving?"

"Very early tomorrow, possibly late tonight. Depends on

your mama. You know how she is. Won't wanna leave unless she's certain the patients are gonna be well taken care of. I might have to drag her away from there."

"We goin' to Gramma's again?"

"Where else. . . . Some folks are stocking up on water and canned goods at the supermarkets," he mentioned as we passed a grocery store.

"Why're they doin' that? If Mayor Nagin tells us to get in our cars to leave, then we have to, right?"

"Some folks don't have cars, Saint."

"Then they could take a bus or a train or a plane, even."

"To where? Some folks got nowhere to go."

"They could go to another city and stay in a hotel." Like Mama, I was trying to problem solve.

"And who's gonna pay for that? Some people got no jobs, others got no money, and when I say no money . . . I mean *no* money. Some people got nuthin' except the clothes on their backs, Saint."

"Money's real important, huh?"

"Yep, but what you do with it is even more important. Most a the people who claim money's not important are folks who have plenty of it. You remember that."

"Smokey said he's been frugal. What's that mean?"

"Means he hasn't wasted his money."

"I've been frugal too," I proclaimed. "And now I have all that money I'd been saving for the clarinet."

"Keep savin', got college to think about."

"That's right, Pops. Juilliard," I reminded him.

"You always had the music in you, even before you could walk. Guess it's right us being here in New Orleans . . . music everywhere. King Daddy Saint . . . he had the music too. He'd sure be proud of you."

My grin was ear to ear.

As I packed, I checked off my list. Then I got to number six—Shadow. Without even asking, I left the house and sped to Miz Moran's. She was, of course, sitting on her porch.

"I came for Shadow," I panted.

"Got loose."

This can't be true. "How?"

She shrugged. "Don't know. Had him on the leash hooked to a tree. Only-est thing I could figure is someone musta come into my yard while I was on the toilet and let him go. I am truly sorry." She handed me a paper bag.

"What's this?" I asked.

"The muzzle, leash, and leftover dog food."

No way, I thought, after all my planning and scheming. There were only two words to describe the situation, as MonaLisa would say—booty cheddar. Shadow had managed to get away and I somehow knew that he hadn't needed any help. "I give up."

"You'll find him. I just know it," she said hopefully. "You hurry home now."

"You changed your mind about evacuating?" I asked.

"Nosiree."

"But . . . ?"

Miz Moran patted my shoulder. "Bye, Mister Saint."

"Bye, Miz Moran." I hung my head and plodded home.

The look on my face must have shown exactly how I felt—sadly defeated—because Pops patted my shoulder like he felt sorry for me. "Don't worry. Unless they evacuate New Orleans, she'll be back on Monday."

"Who?"

"MonaLisa. Isn't her being gone the reason for the long face?"

I burst out laughing. Here I was starting to think I was grown when deep down inside I was still just a kid who was a lot more worried about a dog than any girl.

Then I heard *him* outside the door, yelping. "Shadow!" I hollered. I butted the screen open. He jumped against me so hard that I fell.

Quickly, Pops put two and two together. "He's why you were upset, huh? Not MonaLisa."

"Yes."

"If that dang dog means that much to you, Saint, he can stay in your room. But if he starts that barkin', he's outta here. You understand?" he added.

"I understand, and thanks, Pops. He won't bark, I promise."

"You finished packin'?"

"Only one more thing," I assured him.

"Get a move on."

"We gonna load the car?" I inquired as I trotted upstairs.

"And put out a welcome sign to thieves? No. We'll leave everything near the back door." Pops glanced at the mantel clock. It was way past lunchtime. "You hungry?" he asked.

The breakfast I'd eaten had been more than enough to feed most people for an entire day, but not me. "Always."

He grinned and headed to the kitchen. "Must be storin' up for your growth spurt. Fish sound good?"

"Very good."

"After lunch we'll get the plywood outta the garage. You can help me board up the windows just in case."

That he asked me to help didn't surprise me because lately Pops has been treating me kind of different. "Startin' seventh grade," he keeps reminding me.

I'm not sure what crossing the line into seventh grade means to adults, but I sure know what it means to me. Seventh grade is the beginning of cool.

In my room, Shadow tried to squirm into the closet with me, but there wasn't enough space, so I pushed him out. "Cut it out." He nuzzled my back and I fell forward. "Stoppit!"

Shadow stuck his snout in the air and howled long and loud.

"Saint!" Pops yelled longer and louder.

I grabbed my money box and dashed to the top of the stairwell. "It was a howl, not a bark!" I hollered.

Pops laughed.

Once downstairs, I gave Shadow a bowl of water and some food. When he finished, I put the muzzle on him. At the sight of that, Pops got wide-eyed and asked, "Where'd you get that from?"

"I have my sources," I confided slyly as I sat down to eat.

He smiled and knuckle rubbed my head. "Love you, boy."

"Love you too," I repeated, and dug into the food.

That afternoon, as Pops and I boarded up our windows, the sound of nails hitting plywood echoed all over Tremé.

On the other side of us, Mr. Quinn, a pharmacist, was busily boarding up his house. He grinned and waved at us with his hammer. And directly across the street at the Tiberons', jazz blasted over the noise of their buzzing saw.

"Katrina. I never heard that name before," I commented to Pops.

"Kinda pretty, isn't it?"

I agreed.

Pops wiped sweat from his forehead with the back of his hand. "Hope to God this Katrina doesn't do much harm."

"Me too."

I handed Pops another nail, then glanced at my palm. No matter how hard I tried, I couldn't put the creepy life line stuff out of my head. Being an only child was something I'd pretty much gotten used to and I hadn't thought about having a brother or sister for a while. "You and Mama still wanna have another kid?" I asked.

"Yep, but so far no luck."

"Luck can change, right?"

Pops chuckled. "Been a long time since we had this conversation—thought you'd decided you kinda liked havin' me and your mama all to yourself."

"Kinda—but lately I've been thinkin' y'all really should have another kid."

"It's still on my to-do list. What you want this time, a sister or a brother?" ·

"Doesn't matter."

Pops rested the hammer at his side and stared at me. "What's wrong, Saint, you lonely?"

I shrugged.

When he hugged me to his chest, tears got in my eyes.

. . .

We'd nailed the last board and Shadow and I were headed inside when Pops informed me that we had more work to do.

"What?"

"Gonna board up Miz Moran's house for her."

"Miz Moran told me she's not evacuating no matter what."

"We'll see about that too."

Tools in hand, we carted the wood to Miz Moran's house. As expected, she was on her porch and met us with a frown.

"What's that for?" she asked.

"You know dang well what it's for." Pops didn't give her time to object. "You got a ladder, Miz Moran?"

"I might."

Pops grinned. "Where is it?"

"Where are most folks' ladders?"

"In the garage," I answered.

Miz Moran smirked. "Smart child you got there, Valentine." She paused, then continued, "I ran my son-in-law off last night when he came to board me up, but judgin' by the look in your eyes, I spoze there ain't nuthin' I can say to get you to go on home and leave me be."

"Spoze there isn't," Pops replied, and headed to the garage.

We were almost halfway through when Perry Tiberon came over to give us a hand. Until his fingers got crooked from arthritis, he played piano for King Daddy Saint at the

Jazz Shack. Pops calls him one cool old white dude. Perry Jr., his grown son, who everyone calls Squirrel because he can shell and eat a bag of peanuts faster than anyone on earth, was right behind him.

Of course, before we could leave, Miz Moran offered us "A little somethin' to eat," which smelled so good, none of us could refuse. And our stomachs were fat and full when Mr. Tiberon pointed down the street. "Think we should board up old Doc Hunt's house, Val?"

Old Doc Hunt, who had no kids and whose wife was dead, had recently been carted off to a nursing home. His was the biggest and prettiest house on the block.

Pops agreed, "I think we oughta."

"Hard work makes time move with dispatch," Squirrel commented as we hammered and sawed. Squirrel is a college professor with a Ph.D.

"And that means?" I asked.

"It makes time move quickly," he replied.

Why couldn't he just say that? I thought. But when I looked at my watch, I had to agree. No matter how he'd said it, Squirrel was right. The work had taken up all of the afternoon.

By the time we were done with Doc Hunt's house, it was dusk. Quickly, I headed to my room to do what I'd been looking forward to all day. Carefully, I removed the Leblanc from its case and ran my fingers over it. I still couldn't believe it was mine. I played a song I knew well, Gershwin's "Summertime." An instrument as sweet as this ought to have a name, I thought. And just like that, I knew. In honor of the man of the flute, I named it Smokey. I played a few more songs, then carefully tucked Smokey away for the night.

Much later, when Mama finally got home from work, the argument began.

I cracked my door and eavesdropped.

Pops was really ticked off. "What do you mean you might not be able to leave tomorrow?"

"We're still working on getting out-of-area hospitals to agree to take our patients if we have to evacuate. Some will need to be airlifted. But every other hospital in New Orleans is doing the same thing. We can't just leave people here. Got women about to give birth, folks recovering from surgery . . . the ICU and CCU are full, several people on ventilators. I can't just leave."

"Let someone else do it, Mercedes! You got a boy upstairs to think about. I'm not goin' anywhere without you. Let the hospital administrators take care of it. It's their job. Me and Saint, we're your job."

That started Mama crying. "No, Val, you and Saint aren't my job!" she sobbed.

Like a torpedo, Pops exploded. "Not your job!"

"That's right. You and Saint aren't my job. . . . You and Saint are my life!"

Instantly, everything got quiet, so I snuck out to see what was going on. Mama was whimpering and they were hugging. Apparently, the fight was over.

Shadow in tow, I crept back into my room. And a bit later, when my head hit the pillow, I didn't know whether we were leaving for Baton Rouge early the next morning or not. Just in case, I kept Smokey and my cash close.

SATURDAY, AUGUST 27, 2005

Shadow woke me by poking the back of my head with his muzzled snout. Because the windows were boarded up, my room was pitch dark except for a teeny beam of light that had let itself in through an itty-bitty hole in the wood. It was morning and hot. The clock read 9:30. "Mama musta won," I told him.

Downstairs, the TV blared and Pops, like a stamp to a letter, was glued to it. I fed Shadow, gave him water, and joined my pops in front of the box. The hurricane with the pretty name was now a Category Three, and the chance of a direct hit on New Orleans was about 30 percent. President Bush had declared a state of emergency in Louisiana, Mississippi,

73

and Alabama, but so far no mandatory evacuations had been ordered.

"Most folks with an ounce of good sense and the means are leavin' soon or are already gone." Pops shook his head. "Your mama's a soft touch," he sighed. "Always been a soft touch."

"Unless you get her real mad," I reminded him.

"Yep."

"If you can't make her leave today, what are we gonna do?"

"We came to a compromise," he said.

"What's a compromise?"

"An understanding. I gave her till three o'clock. If she's not here by then, we're goin' to get her."

"Did she promise?" I asked.

"She promised."

I spent the rest of the morning snacking, practicing some advanced musical scales, and watching both the TV and the clock.

After lunch, Pops, Shadow, and I headed outside for a game of Frisbee and Pops was showing off, doing a back-handed catch, when the Jupiters drove up. Their SUV was packed full. Jupi waved and hollered, "Hey, Saint!"

I responded with a cool-brother nod and went with Pops as he approached the curb. "Y'all leavin'?" he asked.

Do you think they packed up their stuff to stay? I almost said.

Jupi and I must have been thinking the same thing because we both rolled our eyes.

"Yeah, got family up in Waterproof," Miz Jupiter answered.

I chuckled. "Waterproof? Where's that?" I'd never heard of it.

But Pops had, because he answered for them, "Podunk town north of Baton Rouge in Tensas Parish, not far from Natchez."

"Where're y'all headed?" Jupi's father asked.

"To my mama's in Baton Rouge," Pops told them.

"Be safe then and we'll look forward to seein' y'all sometime next week," Miz Jupiter said. They waved and grinned like they were going on a family vacation, and as they sped off, Jupi blew me a kiss.

"That girl's sweet on you," Pops noted.

"I know," I replied.

At 3:05 P.M., I peered into our driveway. Mama's car wasn't there yet. "Pops," I said, yanking on his shirttail, "it's past three o'clock."

"Grab your stuff and c'mon," Pops commanded. And with dispatch, we left.

Right away, Pops called Mama on her cell, but she didn't pick up, so he left a message telling her we were on our way. Hurriedly, we packed the car and drove off. We passed Miz

Moran, who was resting on her porch. She smiled, then waved at us like nothing was wrong and everything was wonderful.

"What about Miz Moran?" I asked.

"Mr. Tiberon already talked to her family. They're comin' after her later today."

"But what if she won't go?"

"She'll go. Now stop your worrying and buckle your seat belt."

As we screeched away, Shadow, minus the muzzle, barked three times. Pops clenched his teeth.

Of course, dogs weren't allowed in the hospital and I had to stay outside with Shadow. Pops directed us to a tree where I was told to stay and keep my eyes on the car in case someone tried to break in. "I won't be long," Pops said.

An hour later, Pops strolled through the automatic doors—alone.

"Thought you had a compromise?" I spouted flippantly.

"Watch your mouth, now," Pops scolded, and made his way to the car. I was right behind him.

"Well?" I asked.

Pops turned on the ignition. "Well what?"

I shrugged. "What's the plan?"

Pops gazed up at the sky. "The plan is we'll evacuate as soon as it's mandatory."

When we got home, we immediately turned on the television. Hurricane Katrina was now being called dangerous. On one channel the weather people were predicting that the storm surge would top the levees. If that happened, most of the city would be flooded. On another channel they said the levees could crack. I was beginning to get worried. Outside, it turned dark and still no Mama.

"Maybe if I ask," I told Pops.

·"Maybe if you ask what?"

"Maybe if I ask her to come home so we can leave, she will."

Pops smiled and handed me his cell. After three rings, Mama picked up.

"Mama, I think we should leave soon. Okay?"

"I'm doing my best, Saint. But try to understand. Some of the nurses are gone, so the ER and ORs are close to shutting down. A lot of other staff members are leaving tonight and evacuation's not even mandatory yet," Mama responded.

"I know, but according to the news, it probably will be tomorrow," I said.

"As soon as it is, we'll leave."

"You promise, Mama?"

"I promise."

"So you're comin' home pretty soon?"

"As soon as I can."

I should have been asleep when Mama finally got home, but I'd intentionally stayed awake. I glanced at my watch. The hands glowed in the dark. Mama's *as soon as I can* was two o'clock in the morning. Because I expected them to have another fight, I stayed awake for a while. But surprisingly, all was quiet in Tremé.

EVACUATE

"Where's Mama?" I asked Pops as I poured milk on my Cheerios on Sunday morning.

"That's a silly question, Saint."

"At the hospital, huh?"

With his eyes on the TV, he nodded.

"The block is pretty much a ghost town," he said. "Only two families left are the Tiberons and us. Perry's tryin' to wait it out. He and Squirrel are holed up over there with a generator and plenty of provisions."

"And Miz Moran?"

"No sign of her. Not on her porch . . . must be gone."

"You spoze her daughter came to get her?"

"I spoze."

Suddenly there was a special news flash. Hurricane Katrina had been upgraded again, this time to a catastrophic Category Five, and was headed straight for New Orleans.

Then it finally happened. Mayor Nagin's worried face was on the screen, ordering mandatory evacuation. "Katrina is a storm that most of us have long feared," he said.

To help people leave faster, Interstate 10 going west was turned into all one way leading out of the city. They did the same thing with Interstates 55 and 59 going north.

"What about folks who don't have a way to get out of here?" Pops asked the TV.

As if Mayor Nagin had heard him, he said the Superdome was being set up as a "refuge of last resort."

Pops flicked off the TV. "Get dressed!" he ordered.

"Okay," I replied, and flew upstairs.

"And hurry!"

The outside of the hospital was buzzing like a beehive, people rushing here, there, and everywhere. No one seemed to be following any rules and traffic was wacko. Some patients were being pushed in wheelchairs to cars and loaded in. Others hobbled out with walkers and crutches. A few waited on benches. Shadow and I were once again told to plant ourselves. Helicopters came and went. Even though there were clouds in the sky, it still was hot and muggy.

As ordered, I was staying put when I noticed a tiny lady

struggling to get an old man who had only one leg into a car. I knew I had to help her. I looped Shadow's leash around the tree and clasped it. "Sit!" I commanded. For once, he listened.

"You need some help?" I asked the woman.

"Lord yes, child," she answered.

"He'll have more room in the backseat," I advised her, and she agreed.

It took us a while, but we finally got him inside. She told me thank you and was about to hop in her car to drive off without the chair.

"What about the wheelchair?" I reminded her.

She motioned. "It's too big. Got no room for it."

"If we fold it up, it might fit," I said, and proceeded to fold it the way I'd seen them do around the hospital.

She opened the trunk and we lifted it in. There was just enough room.

The tiny lady hugged me tight. "You must be some kinda saint."

"I am," I replied. "Saint Beach."

That got her laughing. "Thank you, Saint Beach," she said as she reached into her purse and smashed an almost brand-new twenty-dollar bill into my hand. With a nod of his head, the old man in the backseat also thanked me, and she screeched off into the traffic mess.

For Juilliard, I told myself as I stuffed the bill into my pocket. I wondered how much it cost to go to school there. I already had the grand I'd saved for the Leblanc. New York City, here I come.

I glanced over at Shadow, who was snoozing, then toward the hospital doors, but Mercedes and Valentine Beach were nowhere in sight. I patted the twenty-dollar bill in my pocket and checked out the area. There she was, a really old woman who desperately needed my assistance. Quickly, I trotted over to where she was trying, without success, to get another old lady, who I figured had to be her sister because they looked just alike, into a car.

"Maybe I could help you," I offered.

"My sis had heart surgery just a few days ago. We're identical twins," she told me as we carefully positioned her sister in what little space was left in the car. And when we were done, she called me an angel and slipped me a ten, which I added to the twenty. This being-helpful stuff was really paying off.

I was scanning my surroundings for another generous person in need of aid when someone tapped me on the shoulder. Startled, I whipped around. It was my uncle Hugo.

"Hey, Uncle Hugo."

Uncle Hugo and Pops had the same big smile. "Hey, Saint. You got your things?" he asked.

My mouth was open to ask why when Pops showed up. The expression on his face told me he'd cooked something up and it wasn't tasty. He and Hugo grinned and butted knuckles. "Thanks for helpin' me out," Pops told him.

"Ain't nuthin'," Hugo replied, then added, "but we're in a hurry."

That's when all four of their eyes landed on me. *Oh no, here it comes.*

"Saint?" Pops said.

"Huh?"

"I'm going to stay here with your mama till this evening."

"And?"

"You're leavin' for Baton Rouge with Hugo right now."

"But what about Shadow?"

"I'll take good care of him. We'll bring him with us," Pops assured me.

"No you won't!" I said as I turned to bolt. But before I could get away, Pops grabbed the back of my collar. He yanked so hard that I almost fell.

Pops raised his voice and put his finger in my face. "This ain't no time to play, Saint!" He was more than serious. "I promise . . . I'll bring the dog. But *you* are leavin' with my brother right now."

"But—" I said.

"But what?"

My eyes began to water and my tears flowed. "I don't wanna go with them. I wanna stay here with you," I sniveled.

Right then, the hospital doors opened and out walked Mama. Hoping she would save me, I ran to her. She wiped my tears.

"Don't make me go," I pleaded.

She glanced at my pops. "We made a decision, Saint."

"What about Shadow? You know he can't stand him. I'm not just leavin' him here to drown or something."

With her arm around my shoulder, we headed to the tree Shadow was sitting under and walked him, well, actually dragged him back to where Pops and Uncle Hugo were standing.

"Hugo . . . is there any way y'all can take the dog?" Mama asked.

"Sorry, Mercedes, we ain't got no room for no big-ass dog like that."

"He's not a big-ass dog," I said.

"Watch your mouth, Saint," Pops warned.

"Plus, Kalisha has that crazy cat she won't go anywhere without." Kalisha is my oldest freckle-face cousin. She has two younger twin sisters, Kalinda and Kiley, who always sing along nonstop with the radio. Hugo shook his head. "Sorry, there just ain't enough room."

Mama stared into my eyes. "I give you my word, Saint. As soon as I'm finished here, we'll leave—"

"And Shadow'll be with you, right?" I interrupted.

"And Shadow will be with us," Mama vowed.

Uncle Hugo fidgeted and glanced at his watch.

"Time to go, Saint," Pops said.

I knelt down and hugged Shadow tightly. "I love you, boy," I whispered.

Pops reached for the leash. "Lemme have him, now."

"Okay," I said, but as I released my grip, Shadow pulled away hard, got loose, and ran. "Shadow, come back!" I yelled. Pops and I ran after him, but it was no use. Tired of being in one place for too long, Shadow fled like a bullet.

I tried not to cry, but my eyes began to water, and soon, two trails of tears were streaming down my face.

Pops patted my shoulder. "I'm sorry, Saint."

I jerked away. "No you're not!"

And as I sobbed, I realized that the how-to-keep-Shadow game was finally over and I, Saint Louis Armstrong Beach, was the loser. Maybe I'm not so smart after all.

ON THE ROAD

Like it or not, I was forced to leave with Uncle Hugo. Mama kissed me over and over.

Pops rubbed my head. "I know you don't believe me, but I am sorry. I'll go back to the house and see if I can find him."

"You will?"

"I promise."

"Hi, Saint," my three girl cousins and their mama, Auntie Vi, said as I climbed into their car. The cat was snoozing in a cage beside Kalisha.

"Hey," I replied. "Hi, Auntie Vi," I added as she tilted her cheek toward my lips for a kiss. She smelled like whatever kind of mint gum she was chewing.

"Seems like we ain't seen you in forever," Kalisha declared.

Even if Kalisha did have a stinky cat, I still liked her. I smiled. "For real, huh?"

From where she stood on the curb with Pops, Mama made the sign of the cross and tossed me a kiss. "See y'all tonight," they hollered.

Seconds later, we slowly headed north, away from New Orleans.

"Did I ever tell you we almost named you Katrina?" Uncle Hugo informed Kalisha.

She frowned. "Sure glad you didn't."

"You hungry, Saint?" Aunt Vi asked.

Shadow was gone and I might never see him again. "Naw," I replied.

Auntie Vi turned around. A kind look shone in her eyes. "Your dog will be just fine."

With that, I started crying again.

Kalisha rolled her eyes. "Would you cut it out, Saint? It's just a dog."

Just a dog, huh? Maybe your just-a-stinky-cat needs to mysteriously disappear.

"Be nice, Kalisha," Uncle Hugo warned.

"I am nice. It's bad enough that I'm gonna have to listen nonstop to the *American Idol* twins all the way to Baton Rouge. And now this?"

"Apologize to your cousin," Auntie Vi commanded.

Kalisha pursed her lips tightly.

"Now!" Auntie Vi added.

Her eyes narrowed. "Sorry," she huffed.

"Now, Saint, I'll ask you again. You hungry?" Auntie Vi repeated.

"Yes," I replied.

"You want a sandwich or fried chicken?"

"What kinda sandwich?"

"Liverwurst."

"What's liverwurst?" I asked.

"It's an acquired taste," Uncle Hugo answered.

"Tastes like liver. You won't like it. I promise," Kalisha added.

"Chicken, please."

"All we got are legs and wings."

"A leg, please."

"Want some soda?"

"Yes, ma'am."

Clumps of folks on the side of the road held signs, mostly asking for rides to Baton Rouge, Lafayette, Atlanta, and Birmingham. One said New York City. Another said *Destination: Wherever You're Going—Will Help With Gas*. A group of men on bicycles zoomed past. I looked up. More clouds were filling the sky.

Kalinda, one of the wannabe singers, proclaimed, "I gotta pee, bad!"

"What'd I tell you about sayin' *pee?*" Auntie Vi scolded.

"I havta go to the restroom, like, right now. Is that better?" she sassed.

"Don't you start with me, Kalinda," Auntie Vi warned her.

Luckily there was a gas station straight ahead and everyone was told to get out and use the facilities, whether they had to or not, because this was the last time we were stopping until we got to Gramma Beach's house.

Instantly, I decided. We'd only come a few miles. It was now or never. As I climbed out, I grabbed my duffel bag and, of course, Kalisha noticed. "We're comin' right back, Saint."

"Where I go, this goes. Got it?"

"Whatever."

As soon as Uncle Hugo went into the men's room, I snuck around to the back of the station and sprinted. There were plenty of trees and bushes, so I had lots of cover and I was sure no one could see me. I ran so fast, my lungs started to burn. Finally, I had to slow to a trot.

That was when I pictured poor Uncle Hugo and Aunt Vi, searching, wondering if somebody had snatched me. Soon he'll be on his cell, talking to my pops. I felt so bad for him. And he couldn't turn back to look for me because both sides of the interstate were one way unless they use the back roads. Those were probably crammed too.

He probably called the police. With everything that was happening, searching for a lost eleven-year-old probably wasn't high on the po-po's list.

Stop worrying, Saint. Pops'll figure out that nuthin' bad happened. That I'm simply an escapee. Before long I'll find Shadow and get back with Mama and Pops where I belong and we'll call Uncle Hugo. Everything's gonna be fine. Just fine.

I ate up the road, and in what seemed like no time, Saint Louis Armstrong Beach was back in Tremé.

Figuring that the Tiberons were still holed up, I had to come up with a strategy. If Perry Tiberon or Squirrel caught wind of me, they'd be on the phone to my pops in a hurry. Then I might never find Shadow. My search for my dog would need to be quiet, especially on my block.

As I made my way down one block and then another, I saw stragglers who'd waited until the last minute to pack their cars to evacuate. Some, like the Tiberons, were staying put, I overheard them brag. Others were going to the Superdome, just in case. One woman, cradling a tiny baby, was walking there. Most of the houses were vacant. Some were boarded, some weren't. A helicopter circled above but soon whirled away. Every so often a car rolled by. But mostly it was quiet.

"Shadow . . . here, boy." I whistled. Nothing.

Finally there was only one place I hadn't searched, the block where I live. Shadow must be there. To avoid the Tiberons, I went around to the block that backs up to ours, because the house behind Miz Moran's has a fence with three missing planks and it's very easy to crawl through. Good, it didn't look like anyone was home. As I squeezed into Miz Moran's yard, I lost my balance and fell hard on my butt. For some reason, that got me laughing.

Then I saw her—Miz Moran, sitting on her back porch, a metal baseball bat resting in her lap. "What's so funny?" she asked.

"Miz Moran! I thought you were gone."

"You thought wrong." She stared at my bag, then shook the bat at me. "You lootin'? Never woulda thought it."

"I'm not a looter, Miz Moran!"

"Then what you doin' here?"

"I came to find Shadow. Soon as I do, I'm goin' to the hospital with my mama and pops."

"They was all up and down here till half an hour ago. Your mama was cryin' and carryin' on somethin' terrible. I peeked at 'em and was 'bout to ask what was wrong, but I know your daddy woulda tried to drag me away from here, so I didn't. What'd you do, run off?"

I hung my head. "Yeah."

"You get in here right now and call 'em 'fore they lose their minds. And be quick about it so they can't trace the call. Like I told ya, I ain't budgin'. And as soon as you find that dog, you call 'em again and wait for 'em on your front porch."

"All right," I said, and followed her inside.

I hoped she was finished, but she kept rambling. "Just don't let that dog be the death of you, you hear me?"

I took a quick look at my life line. "I don't plan to," I replied as I grabbed the portable phone, pushed in the code on the phone that blocks the number you're calling from, then punched in Mama's cell phone number. It didn't even get a full ring out before she picked up.

"Hello?" Her voice was sad.

"Mama, don't worry. I'm okay," I blurted, and hung up fast.

"You got good sense, Saint?" Miz Moran asked.

"Yeah," I replied.

"Don't seem like it. The guv'ment is tellin' y'all to leave and you come here lookin' for a dog."

Do I have good sense? I couldn't believe this. "I only came back for Shadow, Miz Moran. What about you?"

"What 'bout me? Told you I'm not goin' nowheres. I'm old . . ."

"You should still leave."

Miz Moran glanced away. "If the Lord calls me, I'm ready to meet him. Plus I got everything I need right up there." She pointed up.

"In heaven?"

"No, you goofball, in my attic. It's where I hid when my daughter came for me. Got an emergency kit up there. If this Katrina gets ugly and the floodin' goes high like they claimin', I'll be just fine. Yessir, I will."

"You sure?"

"Lemme tell you something, Mister Saint. I'm prepared for the very worst. My emergency kit got everything: a flashlight, lantern, a box of flare sticks, a few of them solar blankets, plenty water, canned and freeze-dried food—"

"Wow," I interrupted. "You're even a better planner than me. Sounds like you really do have everything you need."

She grinned and continued, "Even got one a them inflatable boats with two oars, a battery-operated fan, baby wipes to wash up, toilet paper, plastic bags to hold my waste . . ."

I really didn't want to think about anybody's waste, especially Miz Moran's, and the look on my face must have told her so, because she instantly changed the subject.

"Here, take these scraps and put 'em outside," she said as she handed me a plate of leftover food. "Maybe your Shadow'll get a whiff and come runnin'."

At least she was trying to help me. "You think that'll work?"

"I do. But if you ain't found him by sundown, I'ma make

you call your mama and that's all I got to say to you 'bout it, cuz I'm tired and fixin' to watch my show and close the screen so flies don't get in."

"Yes, Miz Moran," I said, but just in case she changed her mind and tried to pull a fast one and call my parents, I grabbed her portable phone and hid it inside my jacket.

Once outside, I headed around to her front porch and set the plate and myself down. "Shadow," I called softly. I had to be very careful. Pops had most definitely alerted the Tiberons, and if either of them saw me, I was cooked.

The clouds kept coming, rolling across the sky, the blue slowly disappearing. I'd been in a few bad storms but never in a hurricane. People died in hurricanes. I examined my very short life line and considered calling Mama and Pops right then. But I was pretty scared. Saint Louis Armstrong Beach had pulled some stunts before, but nothing like this. This spelled supersize trouble. I remembered MonaLisa's house arrest. Naw, I'll wait—because if I find Shadow, whatever they come up with as punishment will be a ton easier to deal with. Yeah, I'll definitely wait.

Cautiously, I crept out to the sidewalk and surveyed the block from one end to the other. Like a mall at midnight, it seemed deserted. But just like a mall, it had security guards, Perry and Squirrel Tiberon. I crossed to their side of the street. If I avoided their house and the one right next door,

I could probably make my way to the end of the street without being seen. Then I'd circle and come up the other way, steering clear of the house on that side of them and out of plain sight. I put my plan in motion.

"Shadow, here, boy," I said over and over. No Shadow. I figured I must have said the words *Shadow* and *here, boy* more than two hundred times. Yeah, way more than two hundred. It was almost as if he'd disappeared. By the time I got back to Miz Moran's, I'd pretty much given up. I was ready to call my parents and accept my sentence. But when I went to grab the plate with the scraps from the porch to bring it inside, I gawked in disbelief. The plate had been licked clean. Without thinking, I shrieked, "Shadow!"

Quickly I ran around to Miz Moran's backyard. "Shadow!" I said sternly. "I know you're around here somewhere. I'm leaving in a few minutes. So you'd better come on." Nothing. I hurried inside.

"You have any more scraps, Miz Moran?"

She glanced up from the television. "What happened to the ones I gave you?"

"He ate them."

"So you found him. That's nice. Now call your mama, tell her to come get you."

"I didn't find Shadow . . . but Shadow found the food. This time I'll sit with it and wait."

"What you shoulda done the first time. But you know somethin'?"

"What?"

"Coulda been some other critter ate that food. He ain't the only-est dog in Tremé. You know that, don't you?"

"Miz Moran, can I have the scraps or not?"

"You ain't got to get huffy, little Saint. Look in the icebox. Got some ham pieces I was 'bouta throw out."

I grabbed the bag of ham, said, "Thank you," dashed outside, and settled on the back porch. The sun was just about down, and while I waited for Shadow's return to the scene of the crime, I got drowsy. I was wiped out.

"You tired, ain't you, chile," Miz Moran asked sweetly from the other side of the screen door.

There was no denying it. "Yeah, I am."

"Bring that plate on in here. That dog gets hungry, he'll come scratchin' at my door with his tail waggin' like he always does. I'ma fix you somethin' to eat, and when you're done, we gonna call your mama 'n' daddy so they can come get you, unless they already left New Orleans."

"Left New Orleans? They wouldn't leave without me."

Miz Moran snickered. "You sure 'bout that?"

I nodded.

"Good, cuz I'm just funnin' with you."

I cracked a smile.

"Got some red beans and rice left over from yesterday. You want some a that or somethin' else?"

"Red beans, please."

"And if your dog shows up, I'll do my best to keep him here for you. That all right?"

"Yeah—thanks, Miz Moran."

While I ate, Miz Moran retreated to her reclining chair in front of the TV. By the time I was done, she was out like a light. Quietly, I washed and dried the dishes. It was the least I could do. I reached in my jacket and put her phone back.

"Miz Moran," I said gently, trying to wake her, but she was sound asleep.

I picked up the phone to call, but it just chirped and words lit up saying the battery was dead. It probably needs a few minutes in the charger, I told myself.

I turned down the volume on the TV and plopped on the sofa. Miz Moran was snoring. She sure is nice, I thought. And I was hoping nothing bad would happen to her when sleep triumphed and I snoozed.

DAY ONE OF THE DURING

There was no mistaking the bark that woke me up. It was Shadow.

The TV was off and it was almost pitch dark. Rain was beating the house. I wondered what time it was. It felt like I'd been asleep a long time. I needed to call my mama and pops right away. "Miz Moran," I called out. Nothing. Where was she? "Miz Moran!" I hollered.

"That you, Saint?" she asked drowsily from the other side of the room. She must have slept in her chair.

Who else would it be? "Yes, it's me."

"What you still doin' here? Thought your people came and got you."

"I was going to call, but the phone's battery was dead. I musta fallen asleep."

"Me too?"

Shadow barked over and over and scratched at the back door.

"That's your dog. You can keep him in the service porch."

"But I can't hardly see nuthin'."

"Power's out," she claimed. Then I heard a click and a light, as bright as a candle, shone. "Got these push lights all over the house. Told ya I was prepared."

On my way to the door, I stopped and picked up the phone. Now the line was dead. Great.

Shadow kept scratching and barking. I rushed to the door and he squeezed inside. It was close to sunrise, but the sky was black. The wind was howling and I had to lean into the door to shut it. Shadow, dripping wet, nuzzled my leg and I patted his head. "You sure got me in a bunch of trouble," I told him. He looked hungry. "Stay!" I commanded as I closed the service porch door.

Miz Moran had gone through the house, pushing on this light and that one. I could actually see. I opened the refrigerator and grabbed the ham from last night.

"You have something I can put this in?" I asked.

She rummaged through her cabinets and handed me a plastic container. Lickety-split, Shadow gobbled it up.

"You got a raincoat and some rain boots I could borrow, Miz Moran?"

"For what?"

"I'ma take Shadow and go to the hospital . . . see if I can find 'em."

"You ain't goin' nowheres in all this. It's nasty out there. Water gets too high, it's gonna go overtop them levees. That wind is already blowin' faster'n you can run." She went into the service porch and put a key into the back-door deadbolt, locking us inside. The front door was boarded up. She was now the warden and I was her prisoner.

"But—"

"But what?"

"It ain't flooded yet. If I go now, I could get there."

Just then, a bad gust of wind jarred the house.

"Ain't you had enough trouble? You tryin' to die young or somethin'? I'm goin' to the toilet and I expect you to be here when I get out. You understand me?"

I glanced at my peewee life line and replied, "Yeah, I understand."

While she was in there for what seemed like forever, I wondered if she had a cell phone and asked her when she was done.

"My daughter been tryin' to give me one, but I ain't had no use for it."

Disappointed, I plopped down in a chair and sulked.

"Now, that's what I call a pout. Stop your worryin'. We fine so far, ain't we?"

"Yeah."

"Soon as this little trick of nature is done with us, you'll find 'em if they don't find you first. You got what you come here for, didn't ya?"

I knew she meant Shadow. "Yeah," I replied.

"So try bein' happy 'bout that. I'm gonna have some cereal. May as well use this milk 'fore it goes sour. You want some?"

"Okay."

I'd just swallowed my first mouthful when the wind began to blow harder and faster. Miz Moran's tiny Creole cottage rattled like it was about to fall down. I shuddered. The windows in the house next door hadn't been boarded up. Glass shattered. All around, the rain crashed, fighting like a crazy man with the wild wind. Shadow let loose a howl as long as a yawn.

"Katrina's here!" Miz Moran shouted.

"What do we do now?"

Miz Moran put her arm around me and led me to the front room. "Hope the gal shows us some mercy."

All morning it sounded like the house was going to get ripped to pieces, like the wind was about to blow it and everything in it, including me, clear to another country. Katrina was nothing like a regular storm that gets tired and gives up for a while. Katrina was just like the Energizer Bunny, she never got tired and I mean never. I was scared. Naw, I was terrified. I couldn't sleep.

"The radio," I said. "Where is it? Maybe there's news or something."

Miz Moran handed me the radio. "Here, and make sure you put the batteries in the right way."

Quickly, I clicked the batteries into place, turned it on, and surfed the channels. Loud static, soft static, every kind of static. Part of me got mad and wanted to throw the radio into the wall, but I figured we needed it, so I didn't.

After I'd played with it for another twenty minutes, Miz Moran snapped. "That's enough aggravation for a while."

"You want me to turn it off?"

"Yes indeed. Why don't you read a book or something?"

Though we had some light, the house was way too dark to read. Plus, the rain and wind were pounding so loud, it was even hard to think about much except when was this going to be over.

"I think I'll go check on Shadow," I told her.

"You might wanna say a prayer."

"I will," I promised.

Despite what was going on outside, Shadow was calm. I

nestled on the floor beside him and rambled, "Miz Moran says everything's gonna be fine, so don't you worry. She's survived more than a few hurricanes, so I think she's right. In no time I'll find Mama and Pops and they'll be so glad to see me, they won't even be mad or nothing and Pops will finally let you come and live with us because I'm going to use part of the money I've been saving for the Leblanc to send you to dog obedience school so you can learn how to listen and stop barking all the time. But one day I'm going away to New York to Juilliard to really learn music and you can't come with me, so sorry about that."

Shadow raised his head.

"Don't worry. When I graduate, I'm coming straight back to New Orleans, maybe start my own music school or teach at Xavier or Tulane. How's that sound?" Right then I remembered that dogs don't live as long as most people and I wished I had a brother or a sister. "I can't wait until MonaLisa gets back." Miz Moran's advice to say a prayer rang in my ear, and for the first day in a while I decided not to use my one white lie a day. I folded my hands and kept my promise. "God, if you can hear me over all this racket, please take care of Mama and Pops and MonaLisa. Amen."

"Saint, get up and bring Shadow with you!"

"Wassup?" I asked.

"This Katrina's the devil. Just gettin' her steam. That back door's not boarded up, might give way. C'mon, help me. Grab a chair."

We pushed one chair under the back door knob.

She stood beside the refrigerator. "Help me move this."

"Where to?"

"In front of the service porch door."

I smiled. "Miz Moran, you're not strong enough."

"Don't tell me what I'm not. You gonna help me or not?"

I wouldn't have believed it, but we moved it and butted it against the door.

"There," she said with satisfaction. "Think that'll work?"

"Should."

"Y'all come stay with me in the front room, and bring that newspaper." She pointed to a pile. "That dog needs to go pee or poo, make sure he goes on the paper, not on my carpet. He goes on my carpet, I'll have a fit and put him out, you understand?"

"Yes."

Shadow glanced up at me like he understood what she'd said.

"How long you think it'll last?" I asked.

"Depends. Got quick hurricanes that get it over with fast and slow ones that like to take their time."

"I hope Katrina's a quick one."

"Me too, little Saint . . . me too."

With the back door blocked, I couldn't see outside anymore. "Miz Moran, you think this is what it feels like to be in a submarine?"

"Never been in one, never wanna be in one. Ain't much for water, 'cept to look at it. Cain't even swim."

"I'm a real good swimmer," I bragged.

"That so?"

"Yeah. And when I go to high school, I might try to get on the swim team."

"I'm hungry," she said. "You?"

"What you got?"

"Canned soup—beef or chicken?"

After all the good food I was used to eating, neither sounded very tasty. "Chicken."

I popped the top and ate. It was cold and too salty.

Miz Moran swallowed a spoonful of hers and coughed. "Lord have mercy. Sure could go for some gumbo and potato salad."

I nodded. "Or beans and rice or fried chicken from Willie Mae's."

"Quit it, boy, you makin' my mouth water. New Orleans got the best food, don't it."

"And music."

"Lord, yes. It's got the magic. Nuthin' else like New Orleans." She took another mouthful, then got still. "Listen."

"To what?"

"The wind is slackin' up. If it don't get much worse, New Orleans gonna be okay."

Hoping she was right, I smiled.

Then Miz Moran turned her ear toward the window. "But the water's rising."

Shadow scratched at the door like he wanted out. I couldn't blame him. I did too.

I stopped eating and pulled my duffel bag close.

"What's in there that you can't live without, little Saint?"

"Cash, a lot of it," I said as I unzipped the bag. "And this." To protect it, I'd wrapped it in thick plastic. Carefully, I removed it from its case and held it up for her to see.

"That's a mighty fine clarinet."

"It's a Leblanc L1020 Step-Up Pro. But I call it Smokey because that's the name of the friend who gave it to me," I said proudly. "If you like, I could play something."

"I'd like that."

I put on the mouthpiece, and as I played, old Miz Moran closed her eyes and moved to the music.

Playing the Leblanc started me thinking we just might get out of this mess.

THE WATER RISES

By the afternoon, there was still no water in the house. Miz Moran said that was a good sign.

All of a sudden there was a sound louder than anything I'd ever heard before—like a meteor had crashed or a giant alien spaceship had taken a nosedive.

Miz Moran screamed.

I darted into the kitchen. "What was that?"

"That big tree that was in my backyard musta fell," she said, and she began tugging at the refrigerator.

Together, we moved it, opened the service porch door, and peered out through the window in the rickety back door. Her backyard looked like a lake and the fierce wind was making ripples in the water. Smack dab in the middle was a huge uprooted tree lying on its side. The top of it had crushed the roof of her back neighbor's house in two.

"Lord have mercy!" She shook her head like she didn't believe what she was seeing.

"No one's home there. I checked," I told her.

"Thank God for that." She studied the water. "Just a little more than three feet now. Don't get no worse, New Orleans might make out okay."

"I guess the levees are doin' their job," I said happily as we stepped into the kitchen and pushed the refrigerator back in front of the service porch door.

"Spoze they are."

Suddenly the wind turned gruesome again, and as if someone had blasted it with a cannon, the back door finally blew in. The glass shattered. Shadow flew under the table and Miz Moran held me tight. "I want my mama and pops," I whispered.

As we retreated to the front room, she consoled me, "Now, now."

I was wondering what would happen next when somewhere far-off it sounded like a bomb had exploded—then another.

"What was that?" I asked.

"Cain't say."

But minutes later, when the water started coming in through

the floor and under the doors, rising fast, Miz Moran got frantic. I'd never heard her cuss before, but her mouth got going like a motor. Some were words I was surprised she knew, and she didn't even apologize like most grown-ups do. Once she was done swearing, she took a deep breath and sighed, "The levees. They musta gone and broke. New Orleans is finished."

"What do we do now?"

"Get the dog and c'mon."

I grabbed my duffel bag. "Shadow!" I hollered, but he wouldn't come out from under the table.

"Didn't I tell you not to let that dog be the death of you?"

"He'll come," I argued, then grabbed his collar and yanked hard. "Now!" I ordered. Thankfully, Shadow listened and, with me at the rear, we followed Miz Moran up into her refuge.

"Toasty up here in my little crow's nest, ain't it?"

You would have thought with all the wind that was blowing outside it wouldn't have been hot, but it was.

"Yeah," I agreed.

"Because heat rises to the top, just like cream." She paused and pointed. "See that window right there?"

I nodded. Like all of the windows in the house, it was boarded up.

"There's a little balcony out there. Me and Mr. Moran used to stand out there and admire the view."

Oh no, here we go with old-people memories. I have to stop her now or just like my gramma, she'll go on nonstop. "Can we turn on the fan?" I asked as I eyed it in the corner. "Unless you don't want to burn out the battery."

"Got plenty batteries," she assured me.

I turned it on, sat in front of it, and grinned.

But Miz Moran didn't smile back, and her eyes looked like she wanted to cry. "We gonna get outta this, little Saint. I promise."

In the morning we opened the attic hatch and shined the flashlight downstairs. The water looked knee-deep.

"Close it," Miz Moran moaned. "Mosta my things is ruined."

"You can always get more."

"But I cain't get another house. Where'm I gonna go?"

"Your daughter'll take care of you."

That seemed to calm her down, but right then her face turned pale and she sat down hard on the floor. She looked sick.

"What's wrong?"

"My blood sugar's sky high. I can always tell."

She may as well have been speaking Russian. "Huh?"

"My diabetes. I forgot to take my insulin shot."

I'd heard about diabetes and knew people took medicine for it. "You should take it now."

"I cain't . . . it's in the refrigerator."

The next question I kind of had the answer to, but I asked it anyway. "What'll happen if you don't take it?"

"I'll probably die."

Quickly, I grabbed a flashlight and opened the hatch.

"Saint . . . you cain't go down there," she protested.

I ignored her and went anyway.

Some of the battery-powered push lights were still going, so it wasn't totally dark. Carefully, I lowered myself off the attic ladder. By the time my feet touched the hallway floor, the water was to my knees. One of Miz Moran's wooden chairs floated by, and all around, knickknacks and books sat atop the black water. A pair of saltshakers bobbed. I stepped on something that had sunk, lost my balance, tripped, and nearly fell.

"Be careful! Watch your step!" Miz Moran screamed.

"I will! By the way, what's insulin look like?"

"Two small glass bottles 'bout as tall as your pinkie finger. One says Novolin with a capital letter R. The other says Novolin with a capital letter N. I need 'em both."

Slowly, I waded into the kitchen. Thinking the refrigerator would open easily, I gripped the handle and pulled. No such luck. The water holding it shut was a lot stronger than I was. No matter what I did, I couldn't get it open. Finally, I figured out what I had to do. With all my might I pushed and pushed until the refrigerator fell on its back. The door part was now above water and opened easily.

Unfortunately, everything inside the refrigerator was jumbled. I rummaged through all the stuff until I found one little bottle and then the other. I grabbed a floating plastic grocery bag and filled it with the medicine, cans of soda, a pack of bologna, mayonnaise, and a loaf of bread. Yes! Victory! I liked the way it felt.

"Got 'em, Miz Moran!"

Before I headed back, I made a quick detour to the bathroom and peed in the toilet, which of course wouldn't flush. Oh, well.

I watched as she took a needle out of her emergency kit, filled it with medicine, and gave herself the shot. "Thank you, Saint," she said.

"Will you be okay now?"

"Should be. I'll check my sugar after we have sandwiches. Got an extra machine right here. Now you get out them wet things."

"Into what?"

"There's a bag of my husband's old clothes over there. He wasn't a big man, so something oughta fit you."

Something did, including a pair of his two-tone shoes. These are sweet, I thought.

Inside my head I calculated what day it was—Tuesday. I took out my notebook from my duffel bag and wrote.

Ten places I'd rather be on a Tuesday in the summertime

1. At the pool, diving off the high board.
2. On Moon Walk or in the Quarter, jiving with Smokey.
3. At Willie Mae's Scotch House or the Wing Shack, eating like a pig.
4. At Congo Square in Louis Armstrong Park with Shadow at my side.
5. Sitting on the curb outside Joe's Cozy Corner, enjoying the music.
6. On MonaLisa's back porch, goofing off, hoping she'd kiss me again.
7. Up in my room, playing my clarinet or computer games.
8. Hanging out with Pops while he does odd jobs around the house.
9. Listening to Mama sing along with the radio while she does the dishes.
10. Anywhere but here.

As the afternoon passed, Shadow stayed pretty quiet and I hoped he would stay that way. Mostly I kept my fingers crossed that he wouldn't poop. Just in case, I put down newspaper.

I pointed to a box that had a picture of a boat on it. "Maybe we should put air in the boat," I told Miz Moran. By the way she was acting, I could tell she was feeling better, and I was glad.

"You think we oughta?"

It seemed like the smart thing to do. "Sure," I replied.

I pulled the bright yellow boat out of its box. "Where's the air pump?"

"I don't have no pump. You can blow it up, cain't you?"

"No way. That'll take forever." I continued reading the directions. "This says a foot pump is included."

"Mighta been. Check that box in the corner."

We were in luck. I attached the pump and soon had the boat filled with air. It wasn't big and the stuff it was made out of felt kind of flimsy, but it looked like it would hold the three of us. If we had to, I figured we could lower it into the house, out the door, and row to dry land. There had to be dry land somewhere.

At the sight of it, Shadow, probably thinking it was a toy, got frisky. He pranced over to the boat and jumped inside.

"Get outta there, Shadow!" I yelled. But instead of getting out, he bit into the rim. There was a loud pop and lickety-split, the yellow lifeboat deflated.

My mouth flew open and so did Miz Moran's.

"Oh my Jesus," Miz Moran whispered.

I was pissed. "You are one dead dog," I said as I leaped through the air and grabbed his neck.

"Saint, stoppit! Not like he knew what he was doing. He's just an animal! Hopefully the water will recede and we'll be outta here tomorrow." Miz Moran began panting and put her hand to her heart.

Immediately, I let go of Shadow and turned my attention to Miz Moran. "What's wrong now?"

"Just a little chest pain. It'll pass. If it don't, I'll take a nitro pill."

Please let that not be downstairs.

She must have heard me thinking, because she waved a small brown bottle at me. "I have it right here. Been using it now and then since I had my first heart attack."

"Your first? How many have you had?"

"Three, but they was mild ones."

This is not happening to me. None of this is real. There is no hurricane and I'm not stuck in an attic with a dumb-ass dog and an old lady who might drop dead any minute.

Miz Moran called my name. "Saint?"

"Huh?"

"You okay, son?"

"Yeah, I'm okay."

Outside, the wind seemed like it was letting up a little, but when I lifted the hatch and peered down into the house, the water was a lot higher. A little more and it would be to the ceiling. "About six feet," Miz Moran claimed.

I'm barely five feet tall, I thought, and glanced at the airless lifeboat. I'd never been a nail biter, but I plopped down and began to chew them to the nubs.

"Here," Miz Moran said. "Let's try some of this freeze-dried ice cream. Says it's what the astronauts eat on the shuttle."

Number eleven of places I'd rather be—anywhere in outer space. I tore open the package and took a bite. It tasted just like chocolate ice cream but without the cold. And like hot chocolate without the hot, it wasn't the same. As I sat there, eating make-believe ice cream, I pictured myself in a space suit with a power pack. I imagined pushing forcefully through the boarded-up attic window and making my escape.

ALMOST THE END OF ME . . . OR NOT

A horrible smell greeted me as I opened my eyes. Shadow or someone had pooped. The fan wasn't going and it was way too hot. Even the push lights were out. My stomach got that hard knot inside that comes right before you throw up and I puked, a lot. From somewhere in the dark attic, Shadow howled.

"Lord Jesus!" Miz Moran exclaimed. "You sick?"

I wiped at my mouth with my sleeve. "I dunno . . . the smell."

"Dog musta done his business."

From a teeny hole in the plywood board that covered the window, I saw light. It was morning.

Miz Moran lit the butane lantern and there it was—a huge pile of dog crap. I vomited again.

"Batteries in the fan must be dead." But when she replaced the batteries, it still wouldn't start. "Motor's burned out."

"Sorry," I said, "about throwing up."

"Nuthin' to be sorry about."

First, we cleaned up Shadow's mess and then mine. The attic was just one room, so we bagged it and dropped it through the hatch into the lake of water that had filled the house.

"Got another little fan somewheres," she said as she searched. "Here it is." She popped in the batteries and we had air. In a few minutes, the knot in my stomach disappeared. But the bad smell was going to be around for a while.

"Okay if I feed Shadow a coupla cans of this tuna?" I asked a little later. There wasn't that much food left. I supposed Miz Moran hadn't planned on having to feed anyone but herself.

"One can now and save one later," she advised.

As I fed Shadow, she carefully pricked her finger to get her blood sugar reading. "Dammit!" she blurted.

That could only mean one thing and it definitely wasn't good.

"Four seventy-five."

"Is that really bad?"

She nodded and reached for her insulin bottles. "Dammit!"
Again—not good.

"Almost empty."

"And there's no more, huh?"

"No, I didn't have time to get my refill."

The water was too high to wade through, the lifeboat was
useless, and Miz Moran was out of medicine. I stared at
my palm and tears got in my eyes. My life line looked like
it had gotten even shorter. Was that possible? "No way!" I
exclaimed.

"What, Saint?"

"No way am I dying up here. I'm not even twelve yet. Plus,
I have lots of stuff I wanna do."

Miz Moran stared into my eyes and made the sign of the
cross. "This is not the end of you, Mister Saint. No matter
what happens to me, don't give up. You gonna make it," she
whispered.

That was when I decided—Katrina was not going to be the
end of Saint Louis Armstrong Beach or Miz Moran or
Shadow either. Somehow I was going to get us out of this.
My eyes darted around the room and landed on the window.
That had to be the answer.

"We have to get that window open," I told her.

"But it's boarded up from the outside."

"Yeah, I know, but there has to be a way," I told her as I

twisted the latch and opened the small window. I leaned into the wood with all my might.

"Be careful, Saint. If that wood gives way, you could fall."

For some reason I felt very sure of myself. "I won't fall," I told her. But the piece of wood didn't budge, so I got on the floor and pushed with my feet. The plywood gave a little. "It moved, did you see?" I asked her.

"Maybe if I help?"

Soon Miz Moran was on her back beside me and we were pressing hard when I heard it—a helicopter. "You hear that?" I asked.

Miz Moran smiled.

The copter was getting closer. I jumped up and yelled, "Move out the way!" I backed up to the farthest side of the attic, and like a mad bull I ran full force and butted into the board. If Miz Moran hadn't been there to grab my arm, I would have flown out the window right behind it.

"Whew!"

Together we huddled on the small balcony and Shadow nuzzled between us, sniffing at the air. Compared to what I'd been breathing in the attic, it smelled wonderful. We were out. Free. But the helicopter had disappeared.

"Oh my God," Miz Moran whispered, and put her hand to her mouth. For as far as we could see, water was everywhere. Fallen trees were on their sides. Roofs and huge parts of houses were gone. Cars were turned belly-up. Garbage and debris floated.

"Next time the helicopter shows up, we have to be ready. Where are the flares?" I asked.

She pointed. "Right there." The box was full.

"Put everything you need close by. Okay?" I advised her as I grabbed the box of flares and my bag.

I kept my ears open for the copter, but hours passed and Miz Moran wasn't looking so good. "You're sick, huh?" I said.

"I'll be fine."

I could tell she was lying. Hoping it might make her feel better, I got out the Leblanc and played.

Seven songs later, she told me I really had a gift.

"Smokey says one day I'll be a virtuoso."

"Seems to me you already are."

After a few more songs, I tucked the clarinet away.

In silence we waited.

"Finally!" I hollered, and quickly went onto the balcony. With the cigarette lighter I lit the flare.

Madly, I waved at the helicopter. "Here we are!" I shrieked. Soon Miz Moran joined me and lit another flare. They must have seen us, because they headed our way. Excitedly, I leaped up and nearly fell from the balcony into the murky water. Again, Miz Moran yanked my arm and saved me.

In a flash, the copter was directly overhead. Then, just like you see on TV, this guy was lowered down on a rope thing. We backed inside so he'd have somewhere to land.

The rescue guy glanced up. "We only have room for one more person. Have to come back for one a y'all!"

"Take the boy!" Miz Moran shouted over the noise.

That was when she went squiggly like cooked spaghetti and passed out on the floor.

"She has diabetes and she ran out of insulin! You have to take her to a hospital right away or she's gonna die!" I screamed.

"You okay here for a while?" he asked.

I nodded. "Yeah."

Hastily, he attached himself to her limp body and with her purse around her neck Miz Moran was slowly airlifted. Sadly, I watched as the big noisy bird flew away. "They'll be back," I told Shadow, "I hope."

From the balcony my ears picked up every sound, and as if I were sitting in front of a huge movie screen, my eyes saw it all: torn-up houses, cars scattered every which way, all kinds of stuff drifting in the muddy water, trees snapped in half. A pelican flapped by.

I couldn't see my house, but I figured that like all of the others nearby it was flooded to the ceiling, that Mama's antiques and fancy furniture were ruined. I wondered if the water would ever go back down or stay this way forever. Maybe, like Miz Moran claimed, New Orleans was finished.

Tears filled up my eyes. "Where are Pops and Mama?" I asked the sky. And I was wishing I was with them when I leaned against the railing, fell asleep, and dreamed.

It was Fat Tuesday and King Daddy Saint was leading the Mardi Gras parade. He was really going to town on the trumpet. Louis Armstrong was beside him, grinning. I was on the sidelines with my Leblanc, watching as they strode toward me, and when they got close, I stepped into the street to join them. All of a sudden the parade came to a halt. King Daddy Saint put his hand to my chest and said, "No, little Saint, we ain't nowheres near ready for you yet."

Louis Armstrong waved his handkerchief in my face. "No-wheres near," he repeated.

King Daddy Saint raised the trumpet to his lips, hit a few high notes, then spoke again. "Don't go inside the Dome," he warned.

As if they were lyrics, Louis Armstrong sang, "Don't go inside the Dome."

"Get yourself to the Jazz Shack . . . promise?" King Daddy Saint asked.

"I promise," I told him, and stepped back into the crowd of onlookers.

. . .

Shadow's barking woke me up. "Stay away from the Dome. Get to the Jazz Shack," I echoed drowsily. The Dome? He must have meant the Superdome, the "refuge of last resort."

Suddenly, I heard something. I sprang up and searched the horizon. *Is that what I hope it is?* It was—a rescue copter, headed our way.

Of course I had to shed a bunch of tears and refuse to leave unless they brought Shadow. "He's my best friend," I sniveled, then added my white lie of the day, "Plus, he saved Miz Moran's life." Shadow wagged his tail.

"So he's a hero?" the rescue guy asked, petting Shadow's head.

"Yessir."

The guy cracked a smile. "Okay. We'll bring him."

But just in case the guy tried to pull a fast one, I made him take Shadow up first.

Already inside were a man and a woman who, like me, were tired and very dirty. They didn't say a word, just stared ahead with huge round eyes.

"They're in shock," the man who'd saved me said.

I had no clue what that meant, but I replied, "Oh."

From the copter I could see for miles. "Everything's flooded," I told the rescuer.

"Yeah." He pointed. "But the Quarter's not too bad."

124

I scanned the Quarter; he was right.

"Where you taking us?" I asked.

"To the Superdome," he said.

The Dome? Oh no.

"Can you take me to Tulane University Hospital instead?
My mama's a social worker there. They even have a helipad."

"Nope. Gotta take you to the Dome."

"But I can't go there. I need to find my parents."

"There are people there to help you."

"But—"

"Those are our orders. Sorry, kid."

TO THE JAZZ SHACK

Seems like we weren't out of the copter for even a minute when they whirled off to search for more stranded people. No one seemed to care where I went or who I was with. From a distance, I saw lots of people outside the Dome, some pacing, others sitting, more lying on the pavement. I heard screaming, wailing, and loud talking. And when the couple with the blank robot eyes headed there, I didn't follow.

As almost everyone who lives in New Orleans can tell you, the Superdome isn't that far from the Quarter, not even two miles. "C'mon, boy, we gotta go." I yanked Shadow's leash and headed toward the Jazz Shack.

But after trudging through only two blocks of thigh-high water, my legs turned to jelly and I fell. My duffel bag floated away, but frantically I swam after it and with Shadow's help got to my feet. I needed to take a rest, but there was no place to even sit. Now wet from head to toe, I slogged on.

All around, people were looting and the cops were busy trying to stop them. A spattering of gunshots rang out. Frightened, I wobbled and took another spill. Again, Shadow tugged on the leash and pulled me up. Slowly, I made my way to the sidewalk, leaned against a building, and sobbed. We had more than a mile to go and I didn't think I could make it, but like a tugboat, Shadow led me on.

More looters, cops, stragglers, and newspeople crossed my path. The few who did glance my way *kept on truckin'*, as Pops would say.

Then, up ahead, one of the looters dropped a box of something. I rushed toward it and grabbed it before it sank. Chocolate chip cookies. I ripped it open, chomped, and gave some to Shadow. "We can make it, boy," I told him. His tail wagged.

After that the blocks seemed to disappear. On some there was more flooding and on others it was less than ankle deep. Finally, we reached the Jazz Shack.

Weakly, I pounded on the door. Nothing. So I tried the knob, but it was locked. I put my ear against the thick metal door. No sounds. Shadow barked, and I yelled, "Anybody in there?" Still nothing. "Open up!" I screamed. No one came and I didn't hear any noises from inside. I shook my head. "Stupid dream," I told Shadow. "We would have been better off at the Superdome. C'mon, Shadow." But like a statue he sat in front of the Jazz Shack door. With my last bit of strength, I tugged on his leash. "I said c'mon." Shadow yelped at the door. At that point I got way too tired and sank to the sidewalk in front of the door. Next time I see the po-po, I decided, I'm asking for help.

I was drowsing when I thought I heard sounds from inside the Jazz Shack. Voices. I leaped up. "You hear that?" I asked Shadow. He sniffed at the door and howled. Again, I banged and tried the knob. "Anybody in there? It's me, Saint Beach." With that the door unlocked and cracked open. Instead of a face, I was met with two double-barrel shotguns pointed right at me. Totally freaked out, I froze.

Suddenly, Shadow sped off. "Come back here!" I shrieked, but as I turned to run after him, a hand reached out from the Jazz Shack, and like a sack of potatoes I was dragged inside. "My bag!" I yelled. Another hand grabbed it, pulled it in after me, and shut the door.

It was pitch black and it wasn't just the fact that I was soaking wet that had me shaking like a leaf. But in seconds someone turned on a lantern and I smiled. Our neighbors, Perry and Squirrel Tiberon, were standing right in front of me.

"Fancy meeting you here," Squirrel said.

I counted ten other people inside. All were musicians I'd seen around the Quarter. Before I knew it, I was in dry clothes and canned food and water were being shoved my way.

"I thought you guys were still at your house," I told the Tiberons between gulps of water.

"We were," Squirrel replied, "until it became apparent that the only sapient choice was to surrender the abode."

"That means it was the smart thing to do, right?" I said.

"Precisely."

"How long do y'all plan on stayin' here?" I asked the group.

They glanced around at one another. Finally, one man replied, "In New Orleans . . . forever."

Around the room, heads nodded and someone whispered, "Amen."

It wasn't what I was asking. I meant how long were they planning to stay in the Jazz Shack, but I let it go.

For the first time in a while, my stomach was full, which made my body feel even more tired. I worried where Shadow was and frowned, but when I glanced at my life line, I thought *Ha-ha* and grinned. Then, like a scary movie zombie, I took my duffel bag, wandered over to a cot, and crashed.

HIS NAME IS SHADOW

From a corner a candle shone and the sounds people make when they're sleeping filled the room. I'm not sure how long I'd slept, but it seemed like forever. Light snuck in from little places. It must be morning, I thought.

Before long a few other people were awake and milling around. But when a dog started up outside, barking nonstop, scratching at the door, everyone woke up. I'd know that bark anywhere. It was Shadow. I leaped to my feet.

"That your dog out there?" one of the men asked. He sounded upset.

"His name is Shadow."

"Didn't ask what you named it . . . asked if that's your dog."

"Yes."

"Then see to him or swish him on away. Don't no one else need to know we're up in here."

Perry picked up his shotgun and headed with me to the door. Carefully, he inched it open, and when Shadow stuck his wet snout inside, I saw them.

I couldn't believe my eyes.

Mama and Pops. I tried to talk but no words came out.

Behind them stood this really tall cop who was kind of a friend of theirs.

Then, before Perry could stop her, Mama flung the door wide open. "Saint!" she screamed. Tears ran down her cheeks, her arms circled me, and she covered me with what felt like a hundred kisses. "My Saint," she whimpered. By then I was crying too.

Tears filled Pops' eyes and he hugged me so tight, I thought I'd bust. I was really feeling the love.

The cop's stare settled on Perry's gun, so he put the double-barrel aside and promptly ushered all of us, including Shadow, inside.

Pops flung his arm around my shoulder and Mama held my hand tightly.

The policeman studied the room. A few of the men seemed like they knew him, and one spoke up. "Hey, Mose. How you?"

"Don't ask me that question, Newt. New Orleans gone crazy and I got too much other stuff to worry 'bout, so even though y'all are under orders to evacuate, I'ma pretend I ain't seen none of this. Just here for the boy."

"So we cool?" Newt asked him.

"We cool," Mose replied. "But y'all can't stay up in here much longer. They want everybody out the city."

Total silence.

Mose scanned the room once more. "Mercedes, Val . . . time to go."

I grabbed my bag and waved. "Bye, y'all."

"Nice boy y'all got there," an old man told Mama.

"I'll see you anon," Squirrel muttered.

"That means you'll see us sometime soon, right?" I said.

"Precisely."

Pops gave Perry and Squirrel long bear hugs. "Thanks for taking care of my boy. I owe both of y'all big-time."

Through her tears that were still coming, Mama offered her appreciation to everyone in the room.

Hats were tipped; one man winked.

Swiftly, Perry led us to the back door, but as we stepped outside into the muck, Shadow hesitated in the doorway.

"C'mon, Shadow," Pops told him. Obediently, Shadow followed.

I gazed up at my pops. Did I hear right? He'd never called him by his name before. "Why'd you call him Shadow?"

Pops grinned and replied, "That's his name, isn't it?"

"Yeah, it is."

BATON ROUGE

"How'd Shadow know where your mama and pops were?" Kalisha quizzed.

It'd been a little more than 216 hours since New Orleans had been ordered evacuated. We were sitting in Gramma Beach's kitchen, eating chili dogs and chips, drinking soda, playing a card game called Uno. Of course, I was winning.

"Yeah—how'd he know?" my little twin cousins blurted.

I shrugged. "I dunno. Just glad he did."

Over and over Pops had told the story about how he and Mama were at the Convention Center, showing my picture around, questioning every rescue crew, until they finally came across the ones who'd airlifted me and Shadow from Miz Moran's roof.

"Yeah, I lifted that kid. Dropped him at the Superdome . . . him and the dog," the rescue guy informed them.

And that's where they were headed when Shadow showed up, barking nonstop, tugging on Pops' clothes. It wasn't long before Pops and Mama got the idea. Shadow wanted them to follow him, which they did. But when they got to the Quarter, the story changed. Cops and the national guard weren't allowing access.

"But my boy's around here somewhere," Mama pleaded.

Suddenly, like an angel, their friend Mose tapped Pops on the shoulder. In seconds, they had an escort.

Tirelessly, Shadow led them through the Quarter to the Jazz Shack.

"Tell us about that dream with King Daddy Saint again," Kalinda said.

Kalisha thumped her sister's head. "No way, he already told us a bazillion times."

"Ouch! I'ma tell!" Kalinda whined.

"Like I care."

Shadow sniffed at Kalisha's smelly cat, which was curled asleep in a chair. Startled, the cat woke up, hissed, and pounced toward Shadow, but Shadow was too quick and got away.

Kalisha picked up her cat, cuddled it, then scowled at me. "That dog needs to leave my cat alone!" she screamed.

"That stinkin' cat needs to get a bath!" I replied loudly.

Gramma Beach's house wasn't very big and being cooped up was making us grumpy. I stuffed the rest of the chili dog in my mouth and headed toward the living room.

Mama, smiling, met me in the hallway. "Found Miz Moran."

"How?"

"Used my connections."

"She's okay?"

"Alive and well in a hospital in Atlanta. They've been in touch with her daughter."

When Mama was done hugging me, which lately she was doing way too much, I did something I hadn't done for a while—the Saint Louis Armstrong Beach boogie.

But when I got to the living room, the other grown-ups were stationed in front of the blaring TV. Pictures of Katrina victims and hurricane damage flashed. Quickly, I lost the happiness.

My gramma shook her head. "It's a shame how they treated those people. Worse than animals."

Uncle Hugo, Auntie Vi, and Pops agreed.

I couldn't watch any more. It was too sad. I grabbed my clarinet and headed outside to the garden. Of course, Shadow tagged along.

A bird with a yellow belly was having fun in the birdbath,

some bees were buzzing, and a dragonfly zipped by. I plopped on the grass, leaned against a tree, and petted Shadow's head.

I'd promised myself, no matter what, that I'd find some way to get in touch with MonaLisa. I wondered if I'd ever see Jupi, the Tiberons, or Smokey again. Would my feet ever walk down St. Bernard Avenue, Canal Street, along Moon Walk, or through the Quarter? Maybe I'd never hop the ferry to Algiers or shovel red beans and rice into my mouth at Willie Mae's one more time. And the way Mama and Pops were talking, we might never be able to go back to live in our house in Tremé.

But even if, like some people claim, New Orleans is over—no one can ever really take it away, because New Orleans is inside of me, Saint Louis Armstrong Beach, and always will be.

I put the Leblanc to my lips and blew some blues.

acknowledgments

Many thanks to Nancy Paulsen for the gentle care she took with this, my fifth novel. Thank you to my agent, Barbara Markowitz, for her continued support. To everyone at Penguin, thanks loads. Additionally, I give special thanks to my sons, Jordan and Elliot, for their love and kindness and to my grandchildren, Alexandra and Dominic, for keeping me young. And as always, I am most thankful to the Holy Spirit, who with a gossamer touch leads us in the paths of peace.